the CELLAR DOOR

By

BRETT GADBOIS

Illustrated by NICOLAS GADBOIS

To Barry
Enjoy the story
Brett

Copyright © 2010 by Brett Gadbois

First printed in 2010

ISBN: 978-0-615-34731-8

Library of Congress Control Number: 2010923901

Cover art by Nicolas Gadbois

Printed in the U.S.A

BELLTOWN

PRESS

FOR WEBSTER

1

Sam Bixby was a curious boy. He loved to touch things, run his hands over them and feel their texture. When he went with his father to his piano teacher's tiny apartment for lessons he picked up a drum, books from the floor, odd shaped pencils in a glass on the table and plucked an African stringed instrument hanging on the wall until his teacher, a patient grey-haired woman of sixty had to say, "Sam—stop!"

He was a slim, nine-year-old bone-white boy with fine hands, brown eyes and a mop of wavy, copper-colored hair. Freckled too. They crept up his hands to his arms and crawled from his feet to his knees. Wherever the sun touched, he was speckled.

Sam's father was named Jack, his mother, Kate. They divorced when Sam was two. The boy had few memories of his parents together.

They lived a short ferryboat ride west of Seattle on Vashon Island. Jack had taken countless fishing trips to northern Minnesota when he was a boy and decided that Sam was finally old enough for them to go together. That summer Jack booked a flight to Minneapolis and rented a cabin on a small lake where the fishing was supposed to be excellent.

When they arrived, Jack rented a car and they took off for northern Minnesota; land of lakes, sky blue water, schools of northern pike, bass, muskellunge and, of course, mosquitoes—millions and millions of them.

"Put down your Gameboy," Sam's father said, when they were fifty miles outside of Minneapolis. "Get a load of this land."

Sam reluctantly turned off the chirping box in his hand and set it on the seat beside him. He had been giving his electronic dog Maisy instructions, teaching her to fetch. He looked out the window. The land was flat with low rolling hills in the distance. They passed by white farmhouses, weathered barns and clumps of huge trees. A flock of ducks rose up out of a cattail marsh like a speckled black cloud.

"We used to come up here when I was a boy," Jack said, nodding to Sam in the back seat. "That's what we did for family vacations—fish."

"Uh-huh," Sam said, glancing at his Gameboy. He longed to pick it up but decided against it. He stared out the window and saw signs for pick-your-own blueberries and a worn billboard with Indians in a canoe harvesting wild rice. There was something about the land that seemed bleak, empty and even a little scary.

A long, silvery lake came into view. There was a figure in a canoe lit from the back, silhouetted. A man, Sam guessed, with an odd, round hat. Something about the figure struck him, as if the fellow was considering Sam from a distance. The man raised his hat in salute and waved, his black arm flapping like the wing of a bird.

"Jeeze," Sam exclaimed, "d'you see that?"

"See what?" his father asked, his eyes on the road.

"Some guy in a boat tipped his hat at me and…and…*waved.*"

Sam's father laughed. "Maybe he knows you. Or maybe you've already made a friend and we're not even there yet."

Sam pressed his nose to the window. His warm breath made a small damp cloud on the glass. He brought his face back from the window and watched the cloud melt. "I dunno...it's weird."

They picked up supplies and food at a local grocery store and made it to the cabin as the sun was setting. Jack unpacked the car, brought their things inside and snapped on the light.

Sam noticed the place was old-fashioned and funky. There were a few beat-up wooden kitchen chairs and a worn-out couch. He zipped around the place touching things, picking them up. He switched on lights, checked the bathroom and bedroom. In the bedroom he found old sportsman magazines on a low table. The covers featured guys bagging ducks on the wing and men landing huge fish leaping out of the water beside their boats. Underneath the magazines he found a treasure—old comic books. *Superman, Batman, Green Lantern* and *Sergeant Rock and Easy Company.* On the cover of that one, Sergeant Rock was braving enemy fire. Explosions were bursting all around him. His face was shiny with sweat, his expression grim. He hadn't shaved in days. "Move out, Easy Company," he growled through clenched teeth.

"Cool," Sam yelled, snatching up the comics and sprinting to the kitchen where his father was unpacking groceries. He plopped in a chair and held up the comics. "Hey Dad, look what I found."

Jack turned and laughed. "Well I'll be. Looks like the kind of stuff I read as a kid. That Sergeant Rock is a tough old rooster. They're fun. 'Course that stuff has nothing to do with real life...those guys never lose. In real life the bad guys win. Not all the time, of course, but plenty."

"You hungry?" Jack asked.

"Nope."

"You probably will be in the morning." Jack slid a pound of hamburger meat into the ancient white refrigerator.

Sam woke to the sizzle of bacon and smell of coffee. He came out of the bedroom in his T-shirt and underwear rubbing his eyes. "I'm hungry," he said.

"Thought so," his father replied, bending over a cast iron fry pan with a spatula in his hand. "Did you have any dreams?"

Sam sat in one of the rickety chairs and stared out the window blinking at the light as if it was the first sunlight he'd ever seen. "I dreamed I was in a boat in the middle of a lake. I'd come from my Mom's and I was rowing to your house. You lived in a lighthouse on the other side. It was getting dark and my arms were tired. I wanted you to turn on your light but you didn't know I was there."

"What happened then?"

"I woke up."

"I guess I better leave the light on all the time."

"Why?" Sam said, blinking.

"So you'll know I'll always be where you can find me, even if your arms are tired."

Jack piled their plates with scrambled eggs, bacon and toast with raspberry jam and brought them to the table. He poured a glass of milk for Sam, warmed his coffee and sat down opposite the boy. They bowed to each other and the food, a ritual they'd observed for years. "Don't just stare at it, Sam, it won't bite you. You've got to bite it."

They ate silently for a few minutes. Finally Sam looked up from his eggs. "What are we gonna do here, Dad?"

His father laughed. "Plenty. Fish. Play cards. Go exploring. Read aloud to each other by the lantern at night. Look for agates. See if we can discover some local critters."

"Snakes?"

"There are probably some snakes around here. No poisonous ones though. Frogs and turtles too. Listen, we're gonna be here a week. I've got some things to take care of today. I need to rent a boat and get the life jackets squared away. You're welcome to come with me if you want, or—"

"What?"

"If that's too boring, you can do a little exploring. But you've got to promise me something."

"What?"

"Stay here by the cabin, OK? I can't have you wandering off. Understand?"

Sam nodded.

"I mean it. If you're not sure, you've got to come with me."

"I'm sure."

His father studied Sam carefully. "Since you like to say 'trust me', I will. But you've got to pay attention and stay close by. OK?"

"Gotcha."

Jack laughed, downed the last slug of his coffee, and got up from the table. He kissed the top of Sam's head, a rat's nest of auburn hair. "I've got *you*, too." He brought his dishes to the sink and ran hot water over them. "Bring your dishes over here, pardner. We've got a big day ahead of us."

Sam brought his dishes to the counter and headed to the bedroom. He came out with comics and sat at the table. His father finished the dishes, wiped his hands on a dish towel and came over to the table where Sam sat. He knelt in front of the boy. "I don't believe I got a hug or a kiss from my favorite son this morning."

"Your *only* son," Sam said, looking up.

Jack wrapped his arms around Sam's shoulders and squeezed. He tried to kiss him on the cheek but missed, and kissed his warm neck. "Both," he said. "My favorite *and* my only." He got up and headed for the door. He turned, framed by the light. "Remember—close by."

Sam heard the slap of the door and looked up to see his father's back grow smaller through the screen. Then he turned back to his comic book.

The Krauts were giving Easy Company what for in the Ardenne forest. Sergeant Rock was pinned down. Things looked grim. A tank burst into flames thirty feet from him. Bill Fredericks was *in* that tank. Something snapped in Rock's head. He'd had it with the Krauts, his commanding officer Morton, that pencil-necked geek, the whole damn enchilada. Bill was a good friend, maybe his best friend. Rock was a man of action and the time for it was now. He jumped out of his foxhole with a Thompson sub-machine gun in one hand and a grenade in the other. "Give me your best shot, you clowns!" he shouted into the incoming fire.

Sam heard a slap and looked up. It was the screen door. Almost as if someone had slipped in. A chill ran up his back. Probably just a breeze, he thought. He stared at something floating behind the fly-speckled screen and recognized it at once from his book: *Insects of North America*. A Zebra Swallowtail butterfly! He left the comic book open on the table, ran to the door and yanked it back. He was outside in a flash. He chased the butterfly across an overgrown lot

through tall dry grass and weeds. Seeds swirled up in his wake. The butterfly sailed over the grass unaware of the boy chasing it. Sam and the butterfly passed into a stand of trees where the air was cool and moist. They came out the other side and continued up a low hill through another grass-covered lot. Sam was winded when he reached the top. He stood there panting as the butterfly climbed higher. He watched until it disappeared into the dark leaves at the edge of the field. The one and only time he'd ever seen a Zebra Swallowtail in his life. "Wow," he said.

His gaze traveled down to an abandoned farmhouse nestled in the hollow below. The walls were standing but the wooden shakes on the roof were gap-toothed and gray. The chimney still stood and there were a few out buildings in various stages of collapse.

He walked toward the farmhouse, passed a metal plow and pounded the seat with the flat of his hand. It made a satisfying *whannng*, sprang back and vibrated with a metal rattle. He laughed.

When he got to the house he noticed the KEEP OUT signs tacked to the chipped white siding. He ignored them and climbed the cement steps to the front door. He opened it and slipped in.

His heart beat faster. He looked over his shoulder through the open door and remembered his father's words, 'close by'. "I'm just gonna take a quick look around, then I'll go," he said to no one.

A nest of mud daubers circled in a corner. Sam stood still until they settled. The place smelled of dry moss and musty linoleum. Flowered wallpaper curled from the ceiling and made its way slowly down the walls toward the floor. There was a dusty plaid couch against the wall. A broken lamp, its shade ripped, leaned over it.

Sam slipped carefully into the living room, testing each board with his feet to make sure they would hold his weight. He walked into the kitchen. The stove was filthy, a cast iron fry pan on one of the rusty burners. There were still plates in the sink. Someone's old white coffee mug sat on the kitchen counter as if they left it there, went out to plow and never came back.

Sam heard a rustle behind him and turned quickly. He glanced at the ceiling. "Yikes," he said, "you *scared* me." A barn swallow had made a nest of mud and straw in the corner. It fluttered at the lip and looked down at him. He paused and heard the high pitched squeaks of baby birds. He studied the nest and could see their beaks moving.

His eyes traveled down the wall and stopped at a circus poster. It was an odd, old-fashioned thing with heavy black type on thick orange paper. The date on it said August 24th. Sam stared. "Wow...August 24th—my birthday." Beneath the words *Coming Soon to a Town Near You* was an illustration of a huge bear with a funny cone-shaped hat riding a tiny bicycle. As Sam gazed at the poster the bear began to move! He pedaled in precise figure eights, head down, concentrating on his feet on the pedals. He didn't notice Sam watching him. Sam was about to say something when he heard a sharp squawk at his back and whirled around. It was a crow at the window, perched on the sill, his beak open, glaring at Sam through one of the broken panes.

"Scoot!" Sam yelled, waving his arms at the bird. The crow leapt from the sill and flapped away. Sam turned back to the poster. It was the same as before, the bear no longer moving. "Whoa," he said, wiping his damp forehead with the back of his hand. "Don't know what the heck's going on here. Must be seeing things. I could swear that thing just came to life."

He shook his head and glanced at the poster one more time. Satisfied it wasn't going anywhere, he turned and walked through the kitchen. There was a staircase leading up to the second floor. Several steps were missing. He decided it wasn't safe and headed down a short hall. Not much in the bedroom. A caved-in dresser. Mattress on the floor. He crossed to the dresser and looked out the window through broken panes at the path he'd made through the tall grass to the farmhouse. He saw insects rising, flying in the morning light. He remembered his father, kneeling on the old linoleum floor after breakfast. His eyes were brown and serious. "Stay close," he'd said.

"Shoot," Sam said, "he might be back with the boat right now. I'll just—" He noticed an old cement path that was overgrown leading to a heavy door. Must be the cellar, he thought. "I'll just check this out and head on back."

He stepped around the mattress, over broken glass and newspapers and took the hallway to the back door. He opened it, stepped lightly on the wobbly wooden steps and descended to the cellar door. The paint on it was almost gone. He grabbed the rusted handle and pulled. It was heavy. He used both hands and put his weight behind it. The door creaked open and then swung back carrying him with it. He let go and pulled his leg back before the door came down with a crack and split in the middle.

"Yeesh," he said. "That was close."

The cellar was dark except for slivers and flecks of light from cracks in the floor and foundation. A cool, moist smell came up from it. He could make out a couple of wooden boxes a few feet from the bottom of the stairs. I'll just take a look, see what's in those boxes and then head back to the cabin, he thought.

He stepped down. His tennis shoe settled on the splintery wood. It creaked. Then another step, then another. His palms were clammy, his breathing quick and short. So far, so good, he thought. Then he lowered his right foot to the fourth step. It was there for a moment, then gone. It gave way to space, falling and blackness. Then a strange, long, floating moment followed by a sharp pain in the middle of his forehead.

2

O uch," Sam said. Lying down, his face prickly, he opened his eyes and saw green. He lifted his head. "Grass—thank goodness. I thought maybe I was—"

"Hah, hah, hah…ouch indeed," a voice said.

Sam sat up and turned his head in the direction of the voice. There was a short, stout man sitting on a split rail fence. He wore heavy brown boots and overalls. His coat was a muddy charcoal gray with a faded white shirt beneath it. His hands were bare but his head was not. Perched atop it was a bowler, faded and frayed on the lid. The chief features of his face were his nose: a bulbous affair, slightly reddish and lumpy as a steamed potato and his eyes, two black marbles set back under doughy brows. Sam felt them on him. The man was smiling and friendly enough, though.

"Where am I?" Sam asked. He stared at the man and his odd hat. "You…look…familiar. Who *are* you?"

"Whoa, sonny. One question at a time. You'll confuse me." He scratched his chin and studied Sam. "I'd say you're about twenty feet away from me give or take a foot." Then he slapped his knee and laughed again. This time he coughed at the end of his laugh. When he was done he looked at Sam. "No sense of humor, eh? Well, you're young. Still got time to get one. I don't believe we've met. This here's my world, your world, our world. 'Course none of us really owns it, you understand. I'd rather not own it. It's enough trouble just to keep my little house swept. I call this place home. You can call it whatever you like: Boneland, Wonderworld, Great Big Hunk O' Rock. Just be prepared to change your mind from time to time."

"Why's that?"

"'Cause the world changes, my boy. Don't want to get left behind, do you? You're young. Can't get ahead of it, but if you run as fast as you can you might keep up with it."

"This looks like my world."

"Looks can fool you. Don't know where you come from. Things show up in my life all the time I never planned; butterflies, insects, clouds, heck—nearly everything. You probably come from someplace where they make fancy footwear." The man nodded to Sam's tennis shoes. "Fine handiwork that. You asked my name. It's Franklin Claypool Duckworth the Third."

"There's three of you?"

A laugh like a dog barking erupted from Franklin's belly. He surveyed his body. "No, only one of me that I'm aware of." He stepped down and approached Sam with his hand extended.

Sam got to his feet, brushed the dust from his butt and shook Franklin's hand.

"Good morning," Franklin said.

"Good morning," Sam replied.

"I've given you my name but I don't have yours," Franklin said, letting go of Sam's hand.

"Sam. Actually, Samuel Bixby."

"OK to call you Sam?"

Sam nodded.

"Well, you can call me Franklin, or Clay, or Duck, or Mr. D. Whatever you like."

"I'll call you Franklin."

"You know, I never asked to be the third of anything. 'Course, I'm glad to be here, glad I was born. Don't get me wrong." Franklin glanced at the boy and smiled. "Food? I suppose you eat food where you come from. Yah hungry?"

"Um, no. I…ate not too long ago. Eggs and bacon. My dad fixed them."

"That's a good man, taking care of his son so's he don't go hungry. Gotta have fuel in the stove. Fire in the engine. If you're not too busy, follow me. I haven't had a bite today. Remember, it's always breakfast somewhere in the world. What with the spinning planet, seasons changing, clouds forming and night becoming day and then spinning 'round again until day creeps into night, says, "Hello, how are you and how about a cup of black tar bitterroot don't you know?"

"What's black tar bitterroot?"

Franklin put his arm around Sam. "C'mon, I'll show you. You're a boy, got the world in the palm of your hand. More energy than you know what to do with. You don't need a cup of liquid sunlight. Black tar bitterroot tea is for crusty duffers like me. Fellas that need a little pick-me-up. It keeps the blood pumping, legs working. Down the path, down the path, down the ever-lovin' path. I'll show you my home. Not much, but it's home and I'd be a fool to complain."

For all his talk of being old, Franklin's step was surprisingly spry. Sam had to walk fast to keep up. The dusty road wound around and snaked back on itself so many times Sam was convinced they were going in circles. They passed beneath towering trees with bright orange butterflies the size of small birds floating by on the breeze. The birds were a curious mix: a long-legged crane-like creature perched on top of a great oak while hummingbirds the size of rabbits buzzed by. Franklin chattered on, pointing out plants that were good for tea, achy legs and sore muscles. Even flowers a person could make into jam if they had a mind to. "Sweet just like they are. Don't need to add honey."

The hummingbirds drowned him out when they flew by. Sam stared at them. He could swear he saw the face of a man on one. His nose a sharp point, mouth tight, concentrating. He longed to point it out to Franklin but the bird vanished and he lagged behind. He stepped up his pace so he wouldn't be left.

At last they came to a curious structure, a small cabin made of odd-sized logs and planks, rough-hewn and handmade. There was a window facing the dirt road. It had neither screen nor glass, just four empty frames. Franklin grabbed the bleached bone handle of the door and pulled. The door didn't budge. He frowned, grunted and tried again, this time harder. The door creaked open. "Never said I was a carpenter." He stepped inside. "C'mon in, don't be shy."

Sam entered the single brown room. There was a low bed, small wood stove and kitchen area with cupboards and counter. Several knives were stuck into the wood planks above it. There was a large urn with a dipper in it for water and a few crude cups made of pinched clay.

Sam noticed a number of wooden masks on the wall by the door. One looked like the head of a boar. Another had a wide, slightly sinister smile like a dark clown. There was a bird-like face with smudged white beak, slanted green eyes, and a half dozen rough feathers springing from the top of its head. The last mask was a frog-like being with bulging eyes, wide nostrils and a broad flat nose. Sam couldn't take his eyes off the masks. It was as if they had some kind of strange magnetic power. Franklin bustled about the place, stoking the wood stove, pouring water into a kettle. He turned and saw Sam staring at the masks. "Some of my friends," he said. "Of course, it's nothing like *being* a frog, or a bird. That requires a heck of a lot more skill and concentration."

"You mean?"

Franklin set the cup down on the counter. "You can be anything you want to be: a butterfly, bumblebee, even a mountain. 'Course, there's the other part too."

"What's that?"

"Letting go. You have to let yourself go completely. Then *you* glide like a butterfly, swoop like a bird. Stand still and vast as a mountain. Nothing like it. Oh… there is one more thing."

"What?"

"You can't stay there. You've got to come back. Back to being Sam. With your interesting shoes and red hair. Back to being a boy about… about…how old are you?"

"Nine."

"Back to being a boy about nine years old."

"Can you show me how?"

"Maybe. We'll see." Franklin took the kettle off the stove and carefully poured the steaming water in his cup. A sharp smoky aroma filled the room. "Ah…black tar bitterroot tea." He sprinkled crushed roots in the other cup and poured water over it. "But this is your cup of tea my friend, a mint root infusion. Much better for growing boys."

Sam smelled something lighter and sweeter, almost green. Franklin handed the cup to the boy. "For you—it's hot. Wait 'til it cools down. I squeezed a bit of lemon and spooned some of the bees hard work in as well. A little honey."

Franklin turned back to the counter and busied himself with breakfast. He said over his shoulder, "Sit down, son. Might as well take a load off."

Sam sat in one of the two rickety wooden chairs. The table was made of thick planks, crude and ill-formed. Sam could see his feet through gaps in the boards.

Franklin hummed as he worked. He cut slices from a chunk of meat on the counter top and slipped them into a cast iron fry pan on the stove where they sizzled and gave off a smoky tang. When the meat was browned, Franklin moved it to the side and cracked two blue speckled eggs on the edge of the pan. They crackled when they hit the hot grease. He glanced at Sam. "Hungry yet?"

"Um, no."

"Suit yourself."

Sam sipped his tea. It was an odd sensation. The tea was hot but not uncomfortable. When it hit the roof of his mouth, he felt as if he'd been lifted off the ground, taken a gulp of high mountain air. Cool and hot. Hot and cool. Then the citrus tang of the lemon with the thick sweet honey taste rolling over it. He'd never had anything like it.

Franklin worked quickly. He wrapped a cloth around the fry pan handle, pulled it from the stove top and scooped the eggs and meat onto a plate. He tossed what looked like a thick stiff pancake on top of the stove, turned it quickly with the knife and warmed its backside, then lifted it with the knife to the counter top. He tore it in half, spread something thick and red that looked like jam on top, brought his plate to the table and sat down.

Sam was about to take another sip of tea when Franklin held up his hand. "Wait," he said. "First a little thanks." Sam set his tea down, his cheeks were warm and flushed. Franklin didn't scold, he lowered his eyes. "Thank you creatures for giving your life, yourselves to us so we can breathe, walk, talk, and carry on. Thank you for sustaining us, letting us live…" he paused, "letting us be friends."

Sam nodded.

Franklin worked at his eggs as if Sam wasn't there. Beads of sweat formed on his brow. After a few minutes he glanced at Sam and set his fork down. "What's troubling you?"

"My father." Sam stared at the table. His watery eyes stung, but he bit his lip and continued, "He told me to stay close and I…I didn't. I wandered off, found an abandoned house, went down the cellar and now…I'm *here*. And I don't know where "here" is. I'm sure my Dad is looking for me by now. I should be back. He's probably worried sick, I—"

Franklin reached over and touched his hand. "You're safe here. Not sure *why* you're here, but you are. Might as well ask the bees why they drink from flowers. Don't know, they just do."

Franklin paused, noticed Sam's puzzled look and continued. "You have a right to worry about your dad. I don't know how you got here and how to help you get back. You can stay here if you want, or you could try that road out there. See where it leads." He nodded to the window.

Sam looked at the four squares of blue and saw an orange bird streak past. He stood up and went to the door to see where it went. It vanished.

Franklin slipped out the door past Sam and stood in front of his house. Sam came out and stood beside him.

"Take this road," Franklin said waving his hand at the dusty path. "Don't know if it will bring you back to your father, but it might. You're welcome to stay here and wait but I can't guarantee he'll show. Don't get many visitors out this way."

Sam had been looking off in the distance to where the road curved and he could no longer see it. When he turned back he started. Franklin's head was frog-like, smooth and green, with eyes the size of ping pong balls and a broad mouth. The rest of his body was the same as it was before. The only thing different was his head. His nostrils flared. He smiled at Sam. Then, with Sam's mouth still open, Franklin's features collapsed into the older man's craggy, familiar face with his bushy eyebrows, dark eyes and black and white stubble on his chin.

"Jeezo peezo!" Sam exclaimed. The hair shot up on the back of his neck and his heart beat like a flag in the wind.

"Like I told you," Franklin said. "You can be anything you want to be."

"Could I do that?"

"Probably. Depends…."

"On what?"

"Your determination. Concentration. Ability to let yourself go. Remember that meat I had for breakfast?"

"Yeah."

Franklin's face began to change. His nose lengthened into a stubby cylinder. His ears grew, narrowed, and came to points. His beard filled out and covered his entire face. His mouth stretched to accommodate the thick ivory tusks pushing over the edges of it.

"Yow!," Sam shouted. "Whoa…whoa…WHOA!" He felt a mixture of awe and fear and thought about running but he was too scared to move.

When Franklin was finished his face was a mass of bristles. "Ahhhh…wild boar for breakfast. Shot him with an arrow myself. I must say, my sense of smell is really something right now." He sniffed the air. "Hearing too. I can smell mushrooms a stone's throw away and hear a butterfly on the wing in that yonder tree."

Then, as if Sam was watching a movie played backwards, Franklin's nose shrank, his ears lowered and rounded and he came back to the face Sam knew. He drew a deep breath, cocked his head to one side and let out a long raspy sigh. "Yep, can't smell near as good now. Definitely can't hear butterflies on the wing. 'Course I'm only showing you a piece of the pie. You can go whole hog if you want to, or, in this case—full boar." He let go with a wild laugh that ended in a snort.

"You mean you could have kept going and had four legs and a tail?"

Franklin nodded. "'Course you've got to make sure you come back. Like I said, you can't stay there."

"Could I do that?"

Franklin smiled. "You could. Don't know if you could in your world. Your dad might get a little peeved if he turns around and finds his son has turned into a wild boar. Go ahead," Franklin hooked his thumb at a passing bumblebee. "Try it."

Sam looked at the bumblebee and imagined buzzing over the leaves and landing in flowers. Nothing happened. He tried again and let go this time. He looked at Franklin and was surprised to see countless Franklins, a kaleidoscope of old men. They were smiling, turning, changing size and shape as he moved his head. Sam saw something long and black directly in front of him. A proboscis!

He looked at his feet and saw countless tennis shoes, knees, and hands by his sides.

"How do you feel?" Franklin asked.

"Like somebody plugged me into a light socket," Sam said. "Part bee, part boy." His voice came out low and rattling. "Like I'm v-v-vibrating."

"You're all abuzz. And probably bumbling too. To bee, or not to bee, that is the question. Only you know the answer, Sam. C'mon back now."

Sam concentrated. His head grew smoother and rounder. His hearing shifted and became less intense. His eyes unified. He focused on Franklin, his craggy face and the sunshine and smile upon it—ear to ear.

"I never…" Sam stammered and shook his head.

"Now you can. Just remember to come back. If you don't, you could spend a lot of time with your nose in the flowers, collecting pollen. Never find your father that way."

"Yeah, I almost forgot."

"So, what'll it be, Sam? You're welcome to stay here if you want. Or...." He glanced at the road.

Sam looked up the dusty road to where it turned. "I don't know which way to go. What if I get lost?"

"Call me."

Sam looked at Franklin in disbelief. "I...I didn't see a phone in your place."

"Don't know about phones, Sam. Think of me. Call my name. *Remember* me." He tapped his chest above his heart. "I'll be right here."

"OK."

"Before you go, c'mon back in. I can't just send you off without a little something."

Franklin darted back into his cabin and busied himself at the counter. He worked for a few minutes slicing and humming, then wrapped his creation in wax paper and tied it with a string. He turned and handed it to Sam. "A sandwich for the road. Can't send you away without something, can I?"

"Thanks," Sam said, taking the sandwich. He stepped through the door. The light was strong on his eyes. He blinked, turned and paused. Franklin stood in the frame. "Thanks for everything."

Sam felt the old man's gaze embracing him, holding him, then letting him go.

"Where am I?" Sam asked.

Franklin looked puzzled.

Sam continued, "I mean if I run into someone and need to ask directions. If I get lost and want to come back. Does this place have a name?"

"Bramblewood," Franklin said. "That's what folks call it. 'Course, me...I call it home."

"Goodbye," Sam said, and turned suddenly. He felt tears welling up in his eyes and wanted to be on his way. He didn't see Franklin wave from the doorway but his goodbye echoed in the old man's sing-song voice over his shoulder.

3

Sam fought the urge to take one last look over his shoulder. He concentrated on his legs moving and the slap of his tennis shoes on the dusty road. He looked around, trying to get his bearings, anything to jog his memory if he needed to come back this way. He noticed a massive oak tree whose roots rippled beneath the lumpy surface of the road. He looked up. A thick cloud of branches climbed skyward. Directly above him was a nest, a family of bright yellow birds. It seemed they were all singing at once. The father, mother and babies. Singing for their breakfast, he supposed. His heart lifted like a leaf on the breeze. He smiled, listened for a moment and moved on.

He felt the pebbles beneath his high-top sneakers as he walked the twisting road. The leafy trees seemed to pulse and keep time with his footsteps. He passed a burst of orange flowers surrounded by bees and green stalks with yellow flowers the size of soup bowls waved near his head. There were bumblebees, spiders, hummingbirds. A twisted, climbing vine looked as if it was choking the life out of a slim young tree. He reached over and pulled. Stems and leaves showered his head.

The vine lay at his feet like a writhing snake. The young tree lifted its limbs as if it was breathing a sigh of relief. Sam could swear it even stood taller.

After walking for several miles he came upon a small stream. A stone bridge rose over it. He was thirsty. He walked down to the waters edge, set his sandwich down and knelt beside the water. He cupped his hand and took a drink. The water was cool and clear and went down his throat like sweet music.

He noticed some blueberry plants growing a few feet away, their fat berries a dusty purple. He picked a handful and popped them in his mouth. They seemed to explode—little round packets of juice. They *tasted* purple. He reached out to pluck some more and noticed tiny blue faces staring back at him. They weren't pleased.

One of the bigger ones glared at him. It had the face of a plump old woman, scowling. "Just what do you think you're doing, young man?"

Sam drew back and sputtered. "Sorry...I thought...I mean...you're *blueberries*. I figured it was OK to—"

"To eat us?" she replied. Her face seemed to swell as if she was ready to pop. "You might have asked, politely. Have you completely forgotten your manners? Maybe you don't have them where you come from."

"I was thirsty. Meant no harm. May I please have some of you... your...berries?"

"Much better," the flustered berry replied. "A young man with manners. So rare these days. Go ahead. We want to be appreciated, you understand. We're not just any old berries, we're blue for goodnes-sakes." She smiled and waited as if that was Sam's cue.

He reached out, plucked her and a handful of other tiny faces from the stems, studied them for a moment and tossed them in his mouth. He couldn't see his mouth turn blue but he felt it. As if some kind of wild purple laughter rippled through his body like the stream at his feet, coursing over every rock.

He looked down at the water and was surprised to see a speckled green trout. It was facing against the current, waiting, probably for unsuspecting insects to come sailing down so it could have a tasty snack.

He gazed at the fish, water rushing over it, its tail waving slightly. He felt his face narrow, grow longer. He could've stopped what was happening to him but didn't. Then, *he* was in the water. It flew past his face like liquid air. He was a fish! The flow of water kept him upright, stable. It held him, carried him, embraced him. As if the water was doing all the work and he wasn't doing a thing. He was swimming as never before. Not like his lessons at the community pool where the instructor had yelled at him, "Keep kicking your legs, chest up!"

Sam watched, mesmerized, as tiny glowing particles shot by on either side of him. Then, a many-legged water insect rippled by on his left. Snap. It happened quickly, before he could think. It tickled his throat and he gulped it down. A frog plopped in the water in front of him. Probably tasty, but a little too big. Then six polliwogs, swimming furiously against the current. They were drifting toward him dead ahead. *Snap, snap, snap, snap, snap, snap.* They were small, smooth and round, a little salty. He swallowed them all.

He saw the sun glint on something up ahead in the water. Light bounced off its delicate wings. It was a green katydid struggling in the current, coming toward him. He opened his mouth and rose to meet it. It was an inch away when he felt something grab his tail and squeeze. He was lifted, coming up out of the water into the great ocean of air. He flipped back and forth trying to see what held him. He caught a glimpse of sharp curved teeth smiling—a raccoon! Now he thrashed in earnest, flipping his body with everything he had. The raccoon tightened his grip and brought Sam higher. Sam leaped with all his might and was airborne—sailing. Then he splashed down in the water with a hard slap.

Concentrate, Sam, concentrate, he told himself. Your heart, your mind, your molecules, your breath. Go, boy, go. He felt himself growing, expanding, rising up out of the water until he was standing in it. Then he was back to his normal size, dripping from head to toe, water running down his face. He stood in the stream almost to his knees, towering over the startled raccoon. Sam glared at the animal and came toward it.

The raccoon's eyes were black and scared. He took three steps backwards, tripped on a rock and fell on his tail. He bounced back up and ran as fast as he could into low-hanging bushes and disappeared.

Sam exhaled a long deep sigh. "Yeeeesh, that was close. I coulda been lunch. Speaking of...."

He searched the bank of the stream and spied his sandwich on top of a smooth flat rock. It looked like the raccoon had taken it, started to open it, and decided to have trout for lunch, perhaps saving the sandwich for later.

Sam shooed flies from the sandwich and picked it up. "Might as well eat this before somebody else does." He sat on a small grassy hump and opened Frank's carefully prepared package. He looked at the round flatbread stained with grease, said, "thanks" softly and dug in.

After chewing for several minutes he felt funny, as if someone was watching him. He looked up. The raccoon had emerged from the bushes. It sat on its hind legs and studied him. It didn't move when their eyes met.

"OK," Sam said, "I can share." He ripped off a chunk of the round bread and tossed it to the raccoon. It landed in the grass about three feet in front of the animal. The raccoon approached the offering carefully, picked it up, sniffed it and tore into it with gusto.

"Lunch," Sam said, taking another bite of sandwich and lifting it, a salute to a fellow traveler. One who almost had *him* for lunch. Sam finished, stood up, brushed the dry grass from his butt and looked at the raccoon. "That's all I've got, you rascal."

The animal stared at him but didn't budge.

"So long, then," Sam said.

He turned and headed over the stone bridge. He looked down in the water for the trout and couldn't see it. The raccoon waited until he was up on the bridge and crept closer to the stream. "Shoo!" Sam shouted.

The animal retreated a few paces and watched him to see if he'd make another move.

"OK then," Sam said and headed down the road to who knows where.

4

Sam knew there were people about, he just hadn't seen any since Franklin. There were plenty of signs of civilization: the handmade stone bridge, the road he walked on and rows of crops he passed by. What gives, he wondered?

He walked steadily uphill from the riverbed and came upon a series of crisscrossed fields that looked as if someone had planted them. There were huge oaks up ahead bordering the fields and split-rail fences along the road.

When Sam reached the oaks he sat down and rested in the shade. He had no idea where he was and decided to ask someone if the opportunity arose. He was thirsty too.

He stood, stretched and followed the road. On a slight rise he saw something peculiar in the distance. It looked like a large high-topped shoe or low boot without laces that had somehow come to rest in the middle of a field. It was almost as tall as the trees nearby. Small figures buzzed around the base. He walked toward it.

The fields on either side of the road were dry and dusty with yellow stalks and stubble rising from the parched earth like a giant's pale whiskers. As he got closer he saw the shoe-like object was a house of sorts with windows and a door.

A boy about Sam's age came running toward him. As he got closer, Sam could see he was barefoot. It didn't slow him down over the uneven ground.

When he reached the fence where Sam stood, the boy stopped and panted with his hands on his knees. Then he straightened up, extended his hand and said, "O'Leary's the name, Terrance. What's yours?"

"Sam Bixby," Sam replied, shaking his hand.

The boy was grimy. He'd outgrown his pants. They rode up above his ankles, frayed at the cuffs. His shirt was patched and worn. It might have been red at one time. Now it was a faded rose. The boy's hair was dark blonde, thick as bristles. His eyes were a startling blue in his sunburned, unwashed face. "Call me Terry," he said, grinning, a gap between front teeth.

Sam nodded.

"Whatcha doing here?" the boy asked.

"Looking for my father."

Sam told Terry about the cellar, bumping his head and meeting Franklin. "My dad and I were going to go fishing," Sam added at the end of his story.

Terry nodded as if he understood but his expression was puzzled. "Sorry to hear about your bein' lost and all. What's fishing?"

"There's hooks and worms and minnows. Rod and reel. You bait your hook, throw a line over the side of the boat and hope a fish chomps it. If he does you pull him up."

"What then?"

"I...guess you cook it and eat it. I've never caught one."

"Oh." Terry scratched his chin. "We catch 'em with these." He held up his hands and smiled. "Those little devils are quick, so you gotta be quicker."

"I'm thirsty. Do you have any water?"

"Sure, c'mon to the house. Ma's there, busy as usual. Got twelve brothers and sisters that I know of. Might be a few more tucked here and there. Cousins that might be brothers. There's a boy named Jody five miles from here looks just like me, spittin' image. Like lookin' in a cracked mirror. Sheesh, he's nutty as a squirrel's nest, though. Climb over the fence, I'll give yah the tour."

Sam climbed over and landed with a soft thud beside Terry.

"Nice shoes," Terry said, staring at Sam's high-tops. "Weird, but nice. Wish I had a pair like that."

Crossing the field Terry said, "We ain't got much, but I can offer you water. That we got."

As they approached Terry's home, Sam saw kids buzzing around the place like bumblebees, running after each other, playing tag, yelping and taunting. An older boy sat at a rough-hewn wooden table outside with a knife in his hand, whittling a chunk of wood. A girl of about six ran past them and screamed, chased by her brother, Sam guessed. The boy chasing her was a year or two older, with a big green frog squeezed in his hand. There was a girl of eight or so with her back to the boys. She was pouring water from a tin can with holes in the bottom of it over a small patch of flowers. Her hair was fine and blonde and seemed to hover 'round her head like a golden halo.

Sam stared at the boot-like structure. There were two floors he could make out. The second floor had a rickety staircase attached to it. The place seemed to be made of hardened mud and straw that allowed for its rounded edges. In fact, there wasn't an edge on the place. Windows bulged from the cracked mud and looked like frog's eyes that might pop out of their frames. The door frame sagged. Terry led Sam inside. There was a stout, apple-cheeked woman standing over a low wood stove. She wore a blue and white kerchief on her head and her skirt brushed the floor. Sweat glistened on her face. She was stirring an enormous pot of steaming clothes with a long wooden spoon in one hand. In the other she held a red-faced wailing baby. She stared at the clothes, ignoring the baby.

"There's Ma," Terry said cheerfully, "doin' the laundry."

"Who's your friend?" she said without looking up.

"Name's Sam," Terry said. "He's lost."

"Is he now?" Mrs. O'Leary replied. "That's a shame. And us without a map. I hope he's not expecting tea. Y'aren't, are you, boy?" She looked at Sam suddenly, surprising him with her blue-eyed stare.

"No...I was just thirsty. I'd appreciate a drink of water."

Mrs. O'Leary made a clucking sound to the baby and it stopped wailing. It gulped and whimpered, churning in her ample arms as if it was swimming on her hip. "Get the boy some water, Terry. He's thirsty."

"Yes Ma," Terry said. He led Sam over to a small hand pump in the corner of the kitchen.

The place was dark and hot. Pots and pans hung from the low ceiling. It was made of mud and sticks, crisscrossed with silvery spider webs. Terry grabbed a clay cup and took a dipperful of water from a bucket beneath the pump.

Sam took a deep drink of water. It cooled and refreshed him as if a mountain stream tumbled down his body from his throat to his toes. "Whoa, thanks." He caught his breath and handed the cup back to Terry.

Sam noticed there weren't any toys in the kitchen. Maybe the kids make do with spoons, pots and pans, a rolling pin, he thought. A few kids ran past the window.

"C'mon," Terry said, "let's go outside. It's stuffy in here."

Sam followed Terry out. Everything looked white without any shadows until his eyes got used to the sunlight. Terry led him over to a home-made picnic table and sat down. The older boy who had been whittling was nowhere in sight.

"I should probably get going," Sam said, sitting on the worn bench.

Terry had a distant look in his eyes. "Yeah...I guess you gotta. I never seen *my* Pa. I asked Ma about him but she don't say nothin'. Just grunts at me. Don't know if he lives close by or way the heck and gone. Shoot, I don't even know if he's alive."

Sam shuddered. "Don't *say* that. My Dad's worried about me, I'll bet." He nodded to the road at the end of the field. "Where's that go?"

"Don't know," Terry said, scratching his head. "I only been a few miles from here. Ma says there's a town with buildings, horses, lotsa people. She calls it Lostville but I never seen it. Said there's a lotta lost souls there. Good place for a boy like me to get into trouble. 'Sides, a fella could have some trouble on the way there."

"What do you mean?"

"I heard stories from my old Uncle Griswold. Says there's robbers, thieves, ne'er do wells. Road pirates he calls 'em. Come in all shapes and sizes. Can't trust a one. And why should he? Says he's been robbed at knife point, beat on, thrown in the bushes, you name it."

"Yikes."

Terry leaned in and whispered, "'Course old Griswold likes to tell a tale. Long and windy stretcher from time to time. Can't believe everything you hear. Likes to drink. I seen him smashed a time or two. Maybe that's how he ended up in the bushes, know what I mean? Now Ma—she warned me there's peculiar folks out there—hybrids she calls 'em. Partials. A little of this and a pinch of that. Fellers with the head of a frog and the body of a man. Snakes that can fly. Weird creatures you never saw the likes of."

Sam squinted at Terry. "You're kiddin' me."

"I'm tellin' yah," Terry answered firmly. "Two-headed monkeys. Bats big as rabbits. Rabbits big as dogs. Ma says she ain't seen all a this, she's *heard*." Terry paused and looked around as if someone was listening. "You don't have to see to believe, you know."

"You're scaring me."

Terry pursed his lips and looked off in the distance. "Why d'you think I stayed so close to home—eh? I know what's good for me."

"I don't have any...anything to protect myself."

Terry's eyes narrowed. He tapped his forehead. "Use your head, sonny boy. Better yet, use your wits. Look at me willya? Yah can't go wrong with that."

Sam looked at Terry and thought, he's only traveled a few miles from home. What would he know about living by your wits? Sam's stomach grew tighter the longer he sat and listened. He felt his forehead. It was moist and warm. He rose from the bench. "Gotta go."

"I'll walk yah to the road."

Sam looked over his shoulder. The blonde-haired girl who'd been watering the flowers was peeking around the house. She ducked out of sight when he saw her.

He turned toward the road and set off with Terry. It felt good to be walking again. His legs were a little rubbery as they crossed the dry stubble. They got to the edge of the field. Sam climbed over the fence. When he was on the other side he turned. Terry saluted as if he was in the army. The army of scruffy boys without fathers, Sam guessed.

Sam raised his hand to his forehead and snapped it back. "So long."

"Don't do anything I wouldn't do," Terry yelled at Sam after he'd gone a ways.

What are you talking about? Sam thought. *Of course I'll do things you'd never do. Can't help it. I'm on the road to Lostville or who knows where. Someplace I've never been and neither have you. Anyway, it's all the great unknown.*

Sam walked the dusty road, his thoughts rattling in his head like pebbles in a tin can. He spied a thick, low tree. Something was odd. A spray of multicolored flowers stuck out from the shiny green leaves. Then the flowers moved. The shy blonde girl from the shoe stepped out. She stood still as a fence post with the flowers out in front of her.

Sam started. "Yeesh—you scared me."

The girl's eyes met his. They were quiet and clear as a pale blue bird's egg. She held the flowers out to him. "These are for you. I grew them myself, watered them. I picked them this morning."

"I...OK...thanks," he said, taking the flowers from her. "I don't know why you'd—"

"Don't let my brother scare you. He likes to talk as much as my uncle. Got loads of stories. A head full of 'em like a hive of bees. I heard you and Terry talking at the table."

Sam looked at her.

"Sorry," she said, "we don't get many visitors." She shrugged and laughed. "OK...we don't get any visitors. After listening to my brother," she shook her head, "he probably scares them all away."

"I'm not so scared now."

"That's why I gave you the flowers. So you'd remember. Not everyone you meet is a bad sort. Sometimes you might even like them. He's right, though. You do have to keep your eyes open. I heard you say you're looking for your father. I had one once I guess. Don't even know if he's the same one as Terry's." She fingered her straw-colored hair, her cheeks flushed and rosy. "Ma likes men and they like her, but they don't seem to stick around for long."

She stared at the ground. She was barefoot like her brother. "I was wondering…can I come with you?"

"I…don't think so." Sam looked up the road to where it curved by two towering oaks. "I'd love to have some company, but I better do this by myself."

"I completely forgot, my name's Nelly."

"Mine's Sam."

She blushed. "I know. I was listening, remember?" She stared at her bare feet and seemed to get shy then. Almost shrink back into the tree. "OK. Can't blame a girl for trying. I did *so* want to have an adventure."

"I'm sure you'll have plenty of those. You look like that kind of girl. Thanks for the flowers." Sam held them up, nodded and started up the road.

He heard her say, "Bye Sam" as he left. It sounded a little odd, high and flute-like. He turned suddenly and looked over his shoulder. He couldn't see her anywhere. There was a yellow meadowlark perched in the short thick tree by the roadside. The bird seemed to glow and pulse on the branch. It was singing with everything it had—its beak, lungs, chest, wings, and legs. Some kind of miniature symphony right there beneath the turquoise sky.

5

Sam walked up one low hill after another. He heard rustling in the tall grass by the roadside. Perhaps mice or squirrels going about their business. He was thirsty again. Large, moist-looking flowers rose up out of the tall grass as if an orange had been cut in half and set on top of a stem. Hummingbirds buzzed down and perched on the lip of the flowers, their wings a blur.

He stood, watched them and concentrated. His heart revved like a motorcycle, picking up speed and whirred like a sped-up watch, ticking, clicking—tick, tick, tick. Then he was on the lip of a large orange bowl—a flower! His wings fanned the air, keeping him aloft. His nose was long and sharp. He steered it to the center of the flower and drank. It was sweet and clear…nectar! Not fizzy like soda pop. The sweetness zoomed behind his eyes and roared in his head.

He heard buzzing, humming. There was another hummingbird right beside him. He glanced over. It looked angry, its green eyes ringed with red. It was buzzing him, nudging him over with its wings. Pushing him away from the flower he was in. He beat back with his wings, struggling to stay upright and keep his balance.

He tumbled over and over and fell in the tall grass. The stems were like tree trunks. There was a ladybug big as a mouse in front of him. A caterpillar the size of a raccoon climbed up a thick stem, slowly, slowly. He could barely move, his wings tangled in the grass.

Something was coming toward him. Dark brown, covered in fur, with a long nose and black eyes. It was taking its time, as if it had all the time in the world.

Why wouldn't his wings work? He beat them like crazy but couldn't lift off the ground. It was the grass, the grass, doggone tall grass.

He brought his attention to the beak in front of him. Concentrate, Sam. C'mon now. Do it. Do it. *Do* it.

He was moving, shifting, coming back to Sam. He heard stems snapping, grass shifting, crackling beneath him. He grew up rapidly like a sapling, strong, swift and true. He looked down at the badger. Its lips curled back in a snarl ready to snap.

Sam brought a low, rumbling growl from deep in his belly. It surprised him that he could make a sound like that. "Arrrgh!" he yelled.

The badger retreated, still baring its teeth, parting the thick grass with its back legs and tail.

Sam lifted his voice higher. "Yarrghh!" he shouted. This sent the animal scurrying back through the tall grass until Sam couldn't see him anymore.

He ran his hand across his wet brow, looked up and down the road to get his bearings and let the air out of his lungs in a deep sigh. "This way," he said to no one. "This is the way I was going."

He stopped beneath one of the two large oaks. He was tired. There was a sunny patch of grass that looked inviting at the edge of the shade. He walked over to it and lay down. The grass was gentle and buoyant at his back. He felt as if the whole world was supporting him. But where was his father? How to reach him? How to get back? Should he go into town? This Lostville place? Maybe his father had returned from his errands, picked up life preservers, supplies, a boat. Maybe he was running around frantically looking for him right this minute. How to let his father know he was OK and trying to get back right now—how?

Sam closed his eyes and remembered his dad. When Sam was five or six they were on a ferryboat crossing Puget Sound from Seattle to Vashon Island. Sam had been drawing cartoons, munching popcorn at a table on the boat. The boat was preparing to dock so they got up and went to the front. A large clump of people had gathered there. He was so excited to see the boat come in he ran ahead of his father into the crowd. He looked over the side at the great swoosh of water below. Its foamy spray. The way it curled, green and white in countless curlicues and bubbles large and small swirling in circles.

When he looked up all he could see were strangers. The people were tall. Businessmen and women coming back from work. Nobody smiling. He saw lots of bellies, shoes and belt buckles. Briefcases, purses, shopping bags, umbrellas, strollers. He figured his dad would be right behind him. He always was. He swung around in the packed crowd—no dad.

There was a voice on the loudspeaker. Someone talking about disembarking the vessel. Then people started moving. Their arms swinging, feet shuffling, boots making thumping sounds on the deck. He heard chunks of conversation. A woman talking about knitting and a man on his cell phone talking about dinner. Still no dad. He couldn't see his father's pale green parka.

He kept moving with the crowd, swept along with them. He wanted to stop. He wanted to ask everyone to stop. He was having trouble breathing, his face hot and sweaty. He felt jittery, as if there were a million tiny hairs in his clothes—tickling him, scratching him, irritating him. He ran back and forth, up and down a long hallway with big windows—still no dad. People kept coming, talking, jostling, moving past him, as if he wasn't there.

Then he was near the door. The crowd separated into two streams.

He could hear cars, traffic whooshing past, getting off the boat.

A woman with grey curly hair stopped and knelt before him. Her eyes were pale blue behind her glasses. She looked at him seriously. "Are you lost?"

Sam nodded, tears swam in his eyes. He shut his mouth tight so he wouldn't cry in front of the strange woman.

"Come over here and tell me your name," she said, taking him by the hand and leading him to the side of the hallway.

He stood for a moment and couldn't speak. It was as if he was coming up from the bottom of a deep lake fighting for air. "Sam Bixby," he said at last, with great effort. "I...can't find my dad."

She led him to a blonde-haired woman with a white shirt standing by a metal box with a phone in it. The only thing Sam could hear was his name. The old woman said it and the woman in the white shirt repeated it. She picked up the phone and spoke into it.

Then Sam heard his name over a loudspeaker. "Will Sam Bixby's father please come to the bottom of the off-loading ramp?"

Sam's eyes searched the people bustling past. Some of them stared at him. Maybe they knew he was lost. He saw his father's raincoat rushing toward him. His dad dropped to his knees and crushed Sam to his chest. "You're here. You're safe. Thank God."

His voice was raw. He was crying. His own father. Right in front of all those people, kneeling on the nubbly grey carpet. Sam held his mouth tight. It quivered like a rubber band. Then he couldn't hold on anymore and let go. He was crying too, his father's arms around him in a great bear hug. He didn't know where his arms stopped and his father's began. His heart seemed to melt into his father's chest. It wasn't his anymore. His father held it, then breathed it back to him. Like he had been underwater and his dad was giving him oxygen, sustaining him, keeping him alive.

Sam could still hear the rustling sounds of people, their footsteps and voices. But none of it mattered. Only being in his father's arms, contained like a ball. A ball that held waves, boats and birds. White clouds floating in blue sky. No edges anywhere.

Sam's dad pulled back, wiped his eyes and then Sam's with the palm of his hand. "Don't ever do that again, OK?"

Sam gripped his father's shoulders and nodded.

6

Sam felt sleepy lying in the fragrant grass. He heard the buzzing of insects. The sun warmed his eyelids. A breeze gently shook the leaves of the big oak. It sounded like the leaves were talking, having a conversation. Whispering secrets to each other. Telling jokes and stories.

He opened his eyes. The clouds above him were rapidly changing, shifting. They formed themselves into pirate ships and dragons. The one directly above him was a giant, fluffy rib cage. Then, he was breathing with the cloud, expanding and contracting, floating off the ground. He'd once seen a kid let go of a red balloon at the state fair. That's how he felt. No more grass at his back now. A breeze supported him. Lifted up his shoulders, arms, back and legs. He rose and fell with the breeze. He turned his head to the right—blue. Then to the left—blue. I must be a cloud, he thought. He let his shoulder drop and rolled over. He no longer faced up. Below him were fields, fences and the tops of trees. He saw the twisting dirt road, squares of green and brown. In the distance the mud-brown shoe house.

To his left a mass of purple clouds rolled toward him. There was a woman's face in them. She was scowling, her cheeks dark. He glanced to his right and noticed a knot of ominous gray clouds approaching quickly. He thought he saw a man's face in them, frowning, then nodding, then laughing. The face had big lips, heavy eyebrows and a shock of wild hair atop his massive brow.

He felt an electrical crackle in the air and heard a snapping, popping sound like a thousand tiny firecrackers going off. It tickled him. He laughed. A wild raspy laugh. Then he spit. His throat was on fire and a bolt of yellow molten energy leapt from his mouth. It blazed down like a fiery root and destroyed a small tree beneath him. There was a great crashing in his ears as the two cloud groups collided around him. Boxing, punching, jostling and butting heads like two huge wrestlers rolling over one another.

He spat again. This time his ragged white-hot root found the great oak below. A big black branch snapped off and fell to the ground smoking.

Then the two clumps of clouds separated and the tickling, crackling electricity disappeared. Space opened up in his rib cage and he could breathe. Then what? He was liquefying. His molecules were getting slippery and running into one another. Sliding together, laughing. This all happened so quickly he couldn't think about it. Could barely keep up with it.

He looked to his right and left. Millions of tiny round faces hummed in the air. Silvery, shiny, clear. Laughing, dancing up, down, do-si-do. Jumping, running, doing somersaults and cartwheels. Spinning round and round. He heard one of the droplets say, "Get ready." Another said, "We're going down!"

One by one they left Sam's side. Dropped from sight. He felt a tap on his back. A big guy, a real drip said, " Hey, buddy—what'cha waiting for? You going down or what?"

"Yeah, sure. Just give me a minute, willya?" Sam replied.

"Suit yourself," the big drop said. "Whatayou think, you're gonna last forever? I'm outta here." Then he jumped.

Sam watched his back until he couldn't see him anymore. Then he felt another tap on his lower back. Sam turned. It was a short drop. He was frowning.

"C'mon, c'mon. What do you think this is, a picnic?" the little guy said. "We got a job to do."

"A job?"

"You kidding?" The little drop shook his head. "Fall—jump—leap—you name it. I don't care *what* you do, just DO it, all right?"

Sam jumped. He looked around. It's as if there was some crazy logic to the drops around him. Just the right amount of space between them. All of them at the right time, the right rhythm. As if they were in some great big dance number where everybody had a part to play.

WHAM! He hit the top of a wide blade of grass and started sliding down. The little drop was at his back. Sam turned. "Hey! Stop pushing, will you?"

"Keep going, keep going," the little guy said. "We ain't there yet. Last one to hit the ground is a rotten egg." Then he laughed, a kind of scratchy laugh like a chicken cackling, Sam thought.

Sam didn't have long to think. He reached the base of the blade of grass and began to sink into the black earth. His heart was beating like the drops thrumming in the grass. He began to dissolve. He saw his father's face. He was worried. Sam remembered Franklin in the doorway of his house. The way he looked when they said goodbye and Sam couldn't look at the man without crying. Then a snapshot of Sam's first steps on the road.

Think, Sam, think. Walk, Sam, walk, he said to himself. First softly, then louder and louder. *Keep talking to yourself, Sam. Keep talking.*

There was a swirling then. A spiral coming up out of the ground. *He* was the spiral, spinning in the wet grass beneath the giant oak. Some kind of miniature cyclone rising up. Then, dizzy from all the twirling, he dropped to the ground in a heap. He was back and completely soaked. A few feet away was the charred limb from the oak he'd hit. Steam rose up from it.

Sam let the air out of his lungs in a long, whistling sigh. He wiped his forehead with the back of his hand. It was no use, his hand was wet too. He laughed and shook his head. "Never get dry *that* way." The rain was easing up. Drops landed in his hair and tickled the back of his neck.

He heard a low sound behind him, rustling leaves. Then muttering, grumbling and growling. As if someone was clearing his throat.

He turned quickly. The great oak was black with rain. He saw a face, old and gnarled in the trunk. Its eyes were capped with thick bark brows. The branches were like great twisting arms.

"Ahem," the tree said.

"Hello." Sam felt a little uneasy at the tree's stare. "That was some rain, huh?"

"Notice anything different about me, young man?" the tree said. Its voice was low and raspy as if it came up from a great hollow log or deep in the earth.

"Uh, no...."

The tree's eyes traveled up its trunk to a raw splintered stump where the branch had broken off. Then its gaze fell on the blackened branch a few feet in front of Sam's soggy sneakers. Wisps of smoke were still rising from the limb.

"Yes, I see. It's really too bad about your arm...I mean limb...I mean—"

"It could've been *me*, you idiot." One of his branches curled out toward Sam. He held the twigs open a few inches apart as if they were fingers. "*That* close. Another foot or two and that would be me lying on the ground. Ever think of that?"

"It wasn't my...my...fault. I was up there." He nodded to the sky. The clouds were parting and he could see patches of blue here and there. "I never meant to get between those fighting clouds...and certainly had no intention of coming down...striking you with lightning.

It's not like I had any choice. You gotta believe me."

"I don't gotta do anything. I ought to teach you a lesson, young man. My daddy never let me get away with that kind of nonsense. He'd have turned me over his knee and given me a planking."

"Planking?"

The tree glared at Sam.

"I never meant any harm, sir," Sam said, taking a step back. "I'm a boy. I'm sorry about your arm, er limb. I don't suppose there's any way I could help you, put it back up there?" Sam nodded to the splintered wood where the branch had been.

The oak shook his leaves gently. They made a swishy, wet sound. A few big drops landed near Sam's feet. His big dark eyes seemed to go back in his trunk. "Nothing you can do now. I can grow another. 'Course it'll take time, you understand. Most everything does these days. Everything worthwhile anyhow." He crossed two limbs and turned thoughtful. "What did you say your name was?"

"Sam. Sam Bixby."

"Reginald Great Oak the Second," the tree said, extending a limb.

Sam drew back, uncertain of the tree's intention. He wasn't sure if the tree would try to grab him and shake him, or worse.

"Go ahead," the tree said. "You humans do like to shake, don't you? There's a thousand ways to say hello. Might as well use the one you know."

Sam extended his hand and took hold of the leafy twigs before him.

They shook.

The tree's craggy face seemed to soften. He smiled.

"I'm looking for my father," Sam said, letting the handshake go. "I'm actually lost. I heard there is a town down this road." He pointed to the muddy lane.

"Father on up the road," the tree said, smiling.

"What?"

"Your father. He might be up this way or not. Don't know who you could ask. 'Course I don't get around much. Just see what I see, hear what I hear. Listen to the gossip the breezes bring me. It's plenty, believe me. Sometimes they whisper so it drives me crazy. Telling me about other places, other worlds. Can't get in a word edgewise, you know? I do need my rest. Although to look at me you'd hardly call it beauty sleep."

The oak shut his eyes for a moment as if he was thinking of something. "Tell you what, I don't know if this will help you or not, but it might." He reached up above his face with one of his limbs to a hollow in his trunk about twenty feet off the ground and plucked something from it. He brought it down and set it in front of Sam's feet spreading it carefully with the twigs at the end of his limb. "A map. It's Chester's, but I don't think he'll mind."

"Who?"

"Chester the squirrel. Like I say, I don't get out much. I'm just plain *out* all the time. Chester fancies himself a world traveler. 'Course I doubt he's ever visited all those places he says he has. He *loves* to talk. Brag is more like it. If he did half the things he said he'd done, he'd probably have circled the globe four or five times."

The map had been folded in the tree. It was creased and stained. What was once white, Sam guessed, was now the rumpled, flecked parchment before him. It appeared to be hand drawn with spidery red and blue lines. Cities were indicated by circles.

"Why is there a hole in the middle of the map?" Sam asked.

Reginald laughed. "Chester. He gets excited. Poked at it one day, jumping up and down like a frog, saying, 'Y'see, y'see—here we are, right here!' Put his finger right through it."

Sam leaned in. "Wow, look at all these towns. Whynot Springs, Oskatoon, Lizards Corners. Pancake Mountain?" He looked up at Reginald.

"It's flat. Don't know why they call it a mountain." He shrugged. "Probably someone was drunk when they named it." He pointed to a small red dot on the map. "Spiderville—now *that's* a nasty place."

"We *need* spiders," Sam protested. "You'd probably be covered in flies without them. My science teacher, Mr. Jenkins told us that."

"OK, OK," the tree said. "Point well taken. They're necessary. I don't have to like 'em though. Lessee, Terrapin City if you like turtles. Hurricane Alley—ummm, pretty scary. I've got relatives that've been knocked over, dragged through the mud, uprooted. Tossed in the air like toys. Some of 'em even blown out to sea."

Reginald looked off in the distance for a moment and then turned back to the map. "Hmmm...here's Tollybrook, Sweltering Heights, Bear Wallow, Porcupine Ridge, No Hope Creek." He paused, "Don't know where this town is you're trying to get to—could be Belltown. It's down the road apiece."

"How far is apiece?"

The tree shook with laughter. "That's what we usually say when we don't exactly know—apiece. Could be five miles, could be ten. Maybe more. Think your father's there?"

Sam looked down the road. The clouds were gone and the sun had returned. "I don't have any idea."

Sam heard a rustling, scratching sound behind him then a small, sharp voice. "What's all this? What's the meaning of this?"

"Uh-oh," the tree said.

Sam turned. It was a squirrel with a russet back and white belly scampering toward him at a clip. He stopped inches short of the map, stood up on his hind legs and pointed to it. "Who did this? This is an outrage. Who's been in my things?" His head jerked back and forth between Sam and the tree. His eyes were glossy and black and his chest puffed out. He was clearly out of sorts. "Well?"

"I was...we were," Sam stammered.

The tree spoke up. "We were looking at your map. I brought it out. If you feel like blowing your cork, blow it at me, OK? And while you're at it, think about finding another place to store your things if you're gonna be a little stinker about this. I'm getting pretty darn tired of—"

"OK, OK," the squirrel said to Reginald. "I can work with this. I mean, I'll do whatever it takes to do the things I need and want to do to make sure that everything and everyone works out alright just the way they should and let bygones be bygones, after all…when a body meets a body comin' thru the rye, I—"

"He's looking for his father," Reginald said, interrupting.

"Well, why didn't you say so?" Chester turned to Sam. "Chester's the name, world traveling's the game." He reached out and shook Sam's hand vigorously. "You need some help with missing persons, stolen purses, lifting curses? I'm your go-to squirrel. Need some know-how, how-to, how 'bout? Heck, *I* can help, got some right here on my top shelf." He pointed to his head. "The universe helps those that helps themselves, what the heck, what the hell. Things are good and even great can'tcha tell? Whoa, Nelly—want me to help you find him? Huh? Huh? I can do it, get right to it, feel it in my tail. It's twitching like a fish on a line. My get up and go is ready to blow—howwww 'bout it?"

"My name is Sam," Sam said, letting go of Chester's hand.

"Pleased to meet you," the squirrel said, nodding like crazy. "Whatayou say, Sam, I'm all caught up in my workaday work load don'tcha know. Got my nuts squirreled away for the winter as they say." He laughed, a dry cackle. "I'm an ace dad hunter, human detector, bad times reflector, good humor infector. Shall we?"

The tree cleared his throat as if he might say something but didn't. He waited.

"Well, I guess so," Sam said. "I could use some help finding this town—this Belltown. And a little company wouldn't hurt either."

Chester jumped on Sam's leg, raced up his body to his shoulder and furiously patted his back. "Atta boy, atta boy, I knew you'd see the wisdom of my—"

Sam leaped two feet in the air from fright and came down with a thud. "Jeeze McGeez!" he yelled. "Watch it, will you? You scared me.

Sheesh."

Chester leaped from Sam's shoulder, landed in the dirt and pawed furiously at his chest as if he was removing invisible dust. He presented a serious face and saluted. "As you wish, sir. First Sergeant Chester Burntside Smally at your service."

Reginald whispered to Sam. "Pssst—he's not really a sergeant. Don't let him fool you."

Sam studied the squirrel still at attention. "At ease, sergeant. Listen, you've gotta be more careful with me, OK? You can't just go running up my leg whenever you feel like it."

"Alright, alright," Chester replied. "If the fit's too tight, don't wear it." He let his arm drop to his side. He looked behind Sam and jabbed the air with his finger, pointing. "Looky there, looky there. I tell yah friends and neighbors, this is a good sign. A mighty good sign. He began to sway to and fro and pat out a rhythm on the grass with his feet.

Sam and the tree looked to where he was pointing.

"A rainbow!" Sam yelled.

"Big as you please," Chester said. "I tell yah fellas, makes me feel somethin'. Somethin' big. Feel like singing." He clapped his hands together softly, got a beat going and began in a clear nasal tone. The great oak kept time scraping its twigs together with a rhythmic snap while Chester swayed back and forth singing:

> Gather 'round me friends
> And I'll give your ears a treat
> It's easy and it's painless
> You'll be rockin' with a beat
>
> If you're lookin' for somebody
> You lost and love so true
> I know just how it feels to be
> So doggone sad and blue

But I'd suggest a better way
A path, a road no less...
It might not bring you fame
Or fortune, even happiness

Take this road before your eyes
Who knows where it leads
Maybe down dark alleys
Or knee-deep in the weeds

You're lookin' for your father
Your mother or your sis
You'd be hard pressed to find
A better road than this

Put your feet upon it
Your heart will lead the way
I can't tell, my new-found friend
If we'll come back this way

We could return tomorrow
Maybe late next week
Might be never, don't you know
So let's be on our feet

I've got to tell you brother
It's a mighty sign
A rainbow to begin this trip
That is mighty fine

Let's get started if you please
Our plans are bound to change

That glowing hoop across the sky
Why...it's as right as rain

The time is now, the road is here
Let's take it 'fore it disappears
My feet are itchin', so's my heart
How 'bout it brother, let's just start

When he finished, Chester stopped, cocked his head toward Sam. "Well...how 'bout it?"

"OK," Sam said. He turned to Reginald. "Sorry about your arm. I never meant to do that."

The tree's limbs waved gently. "I'll have to grow another, or do with what I've got." He extended the tip of his branch to Sam and they shook. "One thing, though...."

"What's that?" Sam said.

"If you come back this way be sure to visit. And, of course if you have some news about your father—"

"We will," Sam replied, glancing at the squirrel who nodded in agreement.

Reginald watched them until they disappeared over the crest of the hill. He sighed. "Youth...always on the go. 'Course if it was *my* father, I'd be looking too."

7

Sam walked with determination. He was surprised that Chester had no trouble keeping up. After a mile or so he wondered if he'd made a mistake bringing the squirrel. He was company, but he was also a chatterbox who just wouldn't shut up. Sam tried gently to let him know. He didn't want to hurt the little guy's feelings. The longer he walked, the more he wasn't sure Chester had any feelings to hurt.

"I got relatives all over the place," Chester said. "High, low, up, down, city folk, country cousins—you name it. My grandfather was a flying squirrel in the air force, highly decorated. He flew campaigns in the bloody battle of Lizards Corners. They threw everything at him: rocks, turnips, carrots, cabbages, twigs, acorns. Heck, even boulders. He was wounded several times. Shot down over Hell's Half-Acre. Left for dead. Rescued by my grandmother, the story goes. She was just a girl then. Took one look at that wounded airman and BAM," Chester clapped his paws together, "true love. Whatever you do, sonny boy, stay away from it."

"Why's that?"

"Nothin' but trouble. Shoot—I've been in love." Chester shook his head. "Her name was Lulubelle. Had a white stripe down her back. The kissing was something else. *Grrrrreat!* Made my tail twitch like a fine watch. That was the good stuff. But after that and the *you* know, there's all that…that…*discussion*."

"Discussion?"

"Yeah. What was right with us. Wrong with us. Mostly what was wrong with me. But back to grandpa. She saved him but did him in as well."

"How do you mean?"

"He was in bad shape—sticks, stones, broken bones, what have you. There was fighting all across the land. She took him in. Had a hollow log fixed up real nice. Gave him hot soup and nursed him back to health. Then they decided to hitch the knot and tie the post."

"What?"

"They got married. Then when the war died down and things got back to normal—well, she loved to cook. I remember going to visit. He could barely get up out of his chair to give me a hug—pitiful. It was like hugging Santa Claus. Only he wasn't jolly, just fat."

"What happened?"

"He never stopped workin', doing stuff around the house. One day she asks him real sweet to grab a tin of acorns on the top shelf. He's up on a wooden ladder. Thing gives way while he's reaching for it." Chester sighed. "That's it. Came down like a box of rocks. Cracked his head and had a heart attack. Never got up. We went to his funeral. 'Course Dad wasn't there. Didn't even show up for his own father's funeral. You're lucky you got a pop, Sam. Lucky I tell you."

"I don't understand," Sam said. "You said he was a flying squirrel. I thought squirrels didn't really fly. They glide, on account of they've got these cool flaps of skin under their arms."

"Details, details. He was *flyin'* I tell yah. All those missions. All those medals. You calling me a blowhard? A talking dummy? Sheesh, he even showed me where he got his leg all dinged up on a night raid

over Alto Formaggio."

"What about your dad?"

They kept walking. Sam glanced at Chester but the squirrel was mysteriously silent. His cheeks puffed and deflated and his whiskers twitched like there was something he was struggling to say.

"Well?" Sam pressed.

"I...uh...don't know what to say. He wasn't around very much if you wanta know the truth. Name's Emmett. Wish I could have tossed the old acorn with him. Or pop one of those boys with a homemade bat." Chester shook his head. "But no, uh-uh, never. Can't do it. Forget I ever asked. A bridge I couldn't cross. A boat I couldn't row. Ma said he traveled a lot."

"Traveled?"

"On business. Had to go check on supplies in other trees. Always on the go. He'd come floating home like a cloud and then slip out the back door like a breeze. Ma said he had girlfriends...rodents on the side. Members of the rat family. 'Course I don't know if they were really rats, or she just said it 'cause she was mad. She was mad a lot. Used to yell at me so I didn't want to spend time at home. I'd hit the dusty road. That's how I got to be, you know, well-traveled."

"Where is he now?"

"Don't know. It's been a couple years since I seen him. Ma passed away a little over a year ago. He used to drop in on her once in a while so if I didn't see him at least I knew he was still rootin', tootin' and rambling 'round. The last time she laid eyes on him she said he looked ragged, like he was on the run from something or someone. Maybe the husband of one of those rats was after him with a carving knife. When you mess around like that you gotta have your bags packed, ready to leave in a hurry."

"And when you saw him?"

Chester frowned and stared straight ahead. "Said he had plans. Not just any plans, mind you—*big* plans. They'd work this time. He had secret information. Whispered as if someone might hear. Something about lost pirate gold. Doubloons the size of your hand. Diamonds big as walnuts. They were guarded but he had it figured out. Hidden passageways and such. He had helpers. Wasn't sure he could trust them, but they were his blood brothers. Probably more like a sack fulla nuts, you ask me."

"Who were they?"

"One was a pack rat, Freddy Skeen. Other guy was a porcupine, name of Archie Bellknap. Porcupines! Look at 'em, you're a smart guy, Sam. Who'd want to get next to those things? Like shaking hands with a thistle, you ask me. As for the pack rat, yeesh, you get any jewels, shoot, anything bright and shiny, they'll stash it somewhere. Never see it again. Might hide gold in the grub they stowed for winter and you'll never find it. You got your doubloons and diamonds mixed in with your nuts. Unreliable at best, downright crazy at worst. Anyway, this was his crew. The guys he trusted."

"Ever find out what happened to him? Did he find the gold, jewels?" Sam wondered if Chester was telling the truth or not. His face seemed too serious to be fibbing for the sake of a good story.

"Not from him. 'Fore Ma died she got quiet about it too. I asked her, pestered her. I know Ma, she was covering. Just shook her head when I asked her if they stole 'em. That's all I got out of her. Had the sense it hadn't gone well. That's the last time I saw her. She died a couple months later. Ma wasn't educated, but she had a kind heart. Left me and my younger brother Roscoe some grub that got us through the next winter. Not sure what we'd have done without it."

Sam glanced at Chester and saw him wipe his eyes with the back of his hand.

"So...you don't know where he is?"

Chester made a circle with his paw. "The big zero—that's what I call him. Captain Chucklehead. He lived high. Sailed like a kite by the seat of his pants until—" Chester shrugged. "Finally, I don't know. Looked for him for a long time. Hit all these towns; Plunkett's Junction, Squigglybrook, Toothless Gap. Even made it to Spiderville. I agree with Reginald Great Oak—it's a nasty place. *Yeesh.*"

Sam started to say something about the finer points of spiders but stopped.

"Anyway," Chester continued, "no sign of dear old Dad. I heard stories; a scrap here, tidbit there, little pieces of a puzzle. One guy said he was livin' large, high on the hog. Another guy thought they'd seen him selling burnt acorns out of a cast iron pot on the muddy streets of Pistol River—*pitiful.* Another story went that he married a princess and turned into a frog. Don't know what to believe, a pack of lies or the holy truth? You tell me."

"Did you give up looking?"

Chester shook his head. "Until I hear for sure, I'll keep my eyes and ears open. Thought I might bump into him. He could be in Belltown. That's part of the reason I came along, Sam."

Probably a big part, Sam thought, though he didn't say. He looked at the road up ahead and realized that the sun was still out but the rainbow had disappeared.

8

They walked past low rolling hills ringed with wood and stone fences. The grass was long and green, its tassels waving in the gentle breeze. Sam was glad Chester didn't ask about his father and mother. He didn't want to explain. Try to make sense of something that made no sense.

His parents had divorced when he was two. He barely had any memory of them together under one roof. He remembered them shouting at one another as he lay beneath the Christmas tree and looked up through the colored lights and branches. He was running his yellow truck through green and red wrapping paper on the floor. Pretending he was digging up dirt, building roads. He remembered after that his father kneeling, telling him he'd be living someplace else and that Sam could come to visit. His Dad took pains to make sure Sam wouldn't feel left behind. Then his father started to cry and apologized all over the place, wiping his eyes with the back of his hand.

Sam told his friend David that he was lucky. "I get two Christmases, two birthdays, get to live in two houses instead of one. Get to go on two summer vacations."

David shrugged and gave Sam a puzzled look like he didn't quite believe it.

Sam's father had a heart to heart during dinner with Sam a month or so before their vacation. Sam's mouth was full of macaroni and cheese and his dad *would* have to bring up something serious to discuss.

"You know your mom wants to move to California," his father said.

Sam nodded.

"I've been fighting it," Sam's father continued, "but I…I lost. She gets to take you this fall if she wants to."

He put down his fork and had trouble talking. Sam looked in his eyes. They were watery. He didn't look back. "I'm sorry," he said, staring at the table.

"It's OK, Dad," Sam replied.

His father explained that his mom could still change her mind but he wasn't holding his breath waiting for that to happen.

Sam remembered walking around his mom's house feeling itchy, prickly, like his skin was hot and uncomfortable and somehow he didn't belong in it. His dog Maisy got into his backpack and scattered papers on the floor. He yelled at her and pulled her tail. His mom sent him up to his room for an hour until he could get hold of his temper. "You've got to calm down," she yelled at him in the kitchen, her face shiny and red.

Chester and Sam walked over a low rise and saw haystacks in the distance. Sam thought they looked like strange, conical bird's nests, only huge. He saw a multi-colored lump at the base of one of the haystacks. When they got close enough Sam could tell it was a figure, wrapped in a dusty plaid blanket. It was moving, adjusting itself as if it was trying to find a better sleeping position. When they got within fifteen feet of it; the figure moaned, cleared its throat and pulled the blanket back quickly, startling them.

"What the—" he said.

He was an odd-looking man. The skin on his face was loose and hung in flaps around his jaw like a bulldog. His eyes were large and blue, set back in his head. They seemed to be slightly crossed, focused in different directions. His mouth was wide and red with thick lips, corners pointing down. His forehead was large, topped by a few wisps of straw-colored bristle, as if some of the hay from the stack had fallen on top of his head and taken up residence there. His body was younger than his face. His face seemed pulled by gravity, as if the earth was tugging at it.

He rose slowly, creaky, and brushed himself off. He wore draw-string pants and soft, moccasin-like shoes. He padded over to Chester and Sam standing by the fence. His odd mouth curled into a lopsided grin. "Rubberface is the name, living's the game," he said, extending his hand.

Sam and Chester introduced themselves and shook hands with

Rubberface. Sam glanced at his face and tried not to stare. He brought his eyes down and studied the flat stones of the low rock wall.

Rubberface noticed Sam staring at the stones and shook his head. "I do a little of this, a little of that and a whole lot of the other. Whatever it takes to get by, you know? You boys look like you're on a journey—an *adventure*." Rubberface held his hand up to his forehead and closed his eyes for a moment. "Don't tell me, let me guess...."

He stroked the loose skin below his chin, peeked at the map sticking out of Sam's pocket and gazed off in the distance. "Hmmm... you're looking for something...or maybe some*one*."

Sam looked up, stunned. He glanced at Chester. The squirrel was surprised too.

"Could be a friend...or maybe relative," Rubberface continued.

"My father," Sam blurted out. "How did you know?"

Rubberface rolled his eyes heavenward as if the answer might be stitched on the underside of a cloud. "Sometimes a man just *knows* things. Doesn't know how or why he knows them, just does." He turned to Chester, "Looking for your father too?"

Chester squirmed. He shuffled his feet, scratching the loose gravel. "I'm *kind* of looking," he mumbled. "Don't know if he's still alive."

"What's his name?" Rubberface asked.

"Emmett," Chester said.

"Only one Emmett I know," Rubberface said. "Last name Smally?"

Chester's whiskers twitched like he bit a lemon. His cheeks poofed out as if he was chewing a mouthful of nuts and working to swallow them all at once. His eyes darted like tiny fish in a stream. He looked like he was having trouble breathing. He said in a shaky voice, "You... know...my...father?"

Rubberface nodded, his expression solemn, mouth set firm like he was thinking of something. "I *did* know him. Haven't seen him in a year or so. Can't say for sure. I know that woman he was with. Name's Florence. Lives up the road not too far from here."

"Would you...could you take us there?" Chester said to Rubberface.

Then he looked at Sam. His eyes were moist. "That is, if it's OK with you."

"Is it on the way to Belltown?" Sam asked Rubberface. "That's where we're headed."

"Don't have a map," Rubberface answered.

"We do, we do!" Chester yelped, jumping up and down. He was so excited he yanked the map from Sam's back pocket and tore it. Sam frowned. Chester gently laid it out before Rubberface, smoothed it with his paw and looked up at Sam. "Sorry."

They knelt over the map. Rubberface ran his finger down the road they'd been on and made little sounds in the back of his throat. "Lessee, right here, yeah, that goes by Pistol River. There's Five Corners. Donnybrook, tough patch *there*. Ummhmm, could be a problem. Whoa, don't want to go there after dark. Good fishing there. Catch 'em with your bare hands. That big oak is on this stretch of road right here—after Five Corners. OK, OK then. I've got it, follow me. He got up, brushed flecks of straw from his pants legs and looked at Chester and Sam expectantly.

Sam glanced at the squirrel and noticed Chester was ready to go. "OK, as long as it's on the way to Belltown."

"It is. I can't guarantee a heckuva lot, but I do know the way," Rubberface said. "We'll just head up this road a bit and then take a shortcut I know. Dips down by a river."

"That's good," Sam said, "'cause I'm thirsty. Sure could use a drink of water."

"You're in luck," Rubberface replied, "'cause that's the name of it."

Sam looked puzzled.

"Thirsty River," Rubberface said. Then he laughed. His cheeks shook like a turkey gobbling.

Sam stared at his grin and the spaces between his teeth. Then he looked up ahead. Chester was setting a brisk pace. He'd have to walk faster to keep up with him.

9

They walked for a few miles. The land was soft and green, with low rolling hills. Rubberface led them down a sandy path to Thirsty River.

Sunlight bounced off the river's surface, dancing and flickering on the water. Sam was mesmerized. It seemed the light and river were playing a symphony. A quiet one, with rushing slides, watery gurgles, rising and falling sighs and faint percussive pops and slaps. The birds were singing over it, with it, through it, adding flute-like trills. Ascending and descending stepladders of bright, clear notes like a string of tiny purple and white flowers hanging in space, suspended briefly, then tumbling down, cascading, falling, coming back up again. Wind played softly in the rushes by the river. A faint sandy rasp along the banks. A rustle of countless notes working together like a broom sweeping a distant room.

Splash!

Sam looked down and saw Chester had jumped in the river and popped back up again, refreshed, bobbing and grinning.

Rubberface knelt at the bank. He slurped noisily from his cupped hands. "Ahhh…now that's right tasty." He wiped his mouth with the back of his hand.

Sam crouched by the river and drank deeply. The water was cold, strong and clear. It flowed to every part of his body. He could feel it saying hello to his blood, making friends with it, shaking hands with it and then dissolving in it until he wasn't separate from the river. The shining wavelets before him had become blood rippling through his body. Going to and fro. This way and that—*waltzing*. On their merry way. Singing, pulsing, laughing. As if somehow the sunlight had entered his body, too. He'd taken a long sweet drink of it. It tickled him. He laughed.

Chester stopped paddling, stood in the water and looked at Sam. Rubberface stared too, from the bank. "What's so funny?" he said.

"Don't know," Sam said, looking past Rubberface at the river. "Nothing I can put into words."

"Humph," Rubberface grunted. "Well, let's hit the road. We're not going to find what you're looking for here." He trudged back up the sandy path and paused at the top looking back at Chester and Sam. "Well…you coming?"

Chester leaped out of the water, shook himself off and sprinted up the path to Rubberface.

Sam took one last look over his shoulder at the river. He whispered, "Thanks" and then headed up the path to join the others.

After they walked awhile Rubberface said to Chester, "So...your father, he had a few friends as I recall...."

Chester nodded, puzzled.

"Packrat by the name of Freddy Skeen and a porcupine, Archie Bellknap," Rubberface continued.

"Why do you ask?" Chester's face knotted-up, puzzled. "Did you know them?"

"We weren't real friendly or anything," Rubberface said. "Didn't know them that well. Had a few drinks in a tavern one night. Haven't seen them in a while. I believe they got into a scrape with the law. Seems there was this...this...*robbery*. Nobody knew for sure who did it, but the police were looking for the three of 'em. I saw posters up all over the place. Your daddy was a wanted man."

"They weren't the only ones who wanted him," Chester said, shuffling along the road.

"I'm looking for him too," Rubberface said. "Wanted to talk to him. Thought maybe I could help him hide out. Him being on the run and all. Might have needed a safe place to stay or hide his goods 'til things cooled down."

Rubberface came to a halt and pointed to a group of buildings up ahead. Chester stopped abruptly and Sam nearly tripped over him. "Up yonder is Five Corners. If anybody asks a bunch of questions like who we are or where we're goin', let me do the talking fellas, y'understand?"

Chester nodded vigorously. He was excited to see the town. His father might be there.

Sam wasn't so thrilled. He wondered why Rubberface was so interested in Chester's father. Maybe he should just leave the two of them and keep going on to Belltown. He didn't know where his dad was, but he wanted to make sure he was on his way to find out.

10

Sam had forgotten how noisy a town could be. The streets weren't paved of course, because there were no cars. There were horses here and there, low wooden carts and an occasional carriage. Some of the horses wore dark squares on either side of their eyes, for what purpose, Sam wasn't sure. People hurried to and fro. The men wore dull-colored coats and pants, the women lighter-colored skirts. Some wore hats and some went without. Some walked in the streets and others stayed on the sidewalks fashioned from rough planks. Their footsteps sounded like clip-clopping hoofbeats.

They passed an odd man in shabby tattered clothes rattling a tin cup. Sam was astonished. The fellow had the body of a man and the head of a monkey. A sad-looking one at that with downcast eyes and long grey whiskers on his cheeks. On top of his head was a faded red cap shaped like a biscuit.

"Spare a few coins, sir? Help a poor fellow out?" he said as they walked past.

Up ahead Sam saw two men unloading wooden boxes from the

back of a low cart. They wore loose-fitting trousers, their shirts soaked with sweat. One had curly blonde hair and a beard. He had a large bright green parrot on his shoulder. The parrot wore a red bandana around his head tied in back like a pirate. The other man was squat and stocky, dark-skinned. He had the body of a man and the head of a dog. His nose was black and moist, brow furrowed, jowls large and fleshy like a basset hound.

The parrot barked orders at the two men as if he was in charge. "You think we have all day? I've got another order to fill when you're done with this. I'm not getting any younger and you're not making much time. Time, time, *TIME!* Once it goes, it's gone, and I do mean gone. Can't get it back no matter what you do. Faster boys, faster. What are you made of—lead? If you can't do this work I can find plenty that can. Plenty, I'll tell you...."

The two workmen barely glanced at the three visitors as they passed by. The parrot followed them with shiny black eyes. "Now *there's* a fine bunch for you: a squirrel, a boy with funny shoes and a refugee from the circus." He laughed, a raspy staccato cackle that sounded like someone hitting a rock with a stick.

When they were out of earshot, Rubberface shook his head and sneered. "Who does he think he is, Mister High and Mighty? Comes into a little money and all of a sudden he's king of the world. I knew him when he was a little Jack Daw scraping to get by. Used to do odd jobs for change and table scraps. He'd repeat whatever you said over and over. Irritating little bugger if you ask me."

"What's going on?" Sam asked Rubberface.

"Don't know what you mean," he replied.

"It's these...these people with the faces of animals. I mean, where I come from nobody has the body of a man and the face of a monkey. Or talking squirrels and trees for that matter. I mean no offense," he added, looking at Chester.

Chester and Rubberface stopped together as if on cue and stared at Sam. "Well shut my mouth and call me Slappy," Rubberface said. He whacked his knee and laughed.

Chester laughed too. "OK, Slappy."

"I guess the joke's on me," Sam said. "You two laugh all you want. I still don't understand."

"We don't know where you come from so we can't compare," Chester said.

"Indeed," Rubberface chimed in. "The ones with the face of an animal and the body of a man are partials, hybrids you might say. A little of this and a pinch of that. That fella back there with the dog face loading boxes might want to be a person someday."

"He could do that?" Sam asked, amazed.

"He could *try*," Chester said.

"Maybe he'd get there, maybe not," Rubberface added. "Some want to and can't get there. Some don't try too hard, comes to 'em effortless, just like that." He snapped his fingers. "As for that insufferable parrot," he jerked his head back, "he probably *wants* to stay a parrot. Likes telling people what to do, repeating himself all the time. Not everyone thinks it's so great to be a human, you know."

"And what's so weird about talking squirrels and trees?" Chester wanted to know, looking irritated. "I can talk and so can you. What's the big deal?"

"I meant no disrespect," Sam replied. He shrugged. "Honestly, I was just curious, I—"

CRASH!

A great clatter came from inside the store directly in front of them. It sounded like pots and pans falling, banging, clanging. The front door flew open. Glass panes rattled in their frames and a squirrel with a worried look and a loaf of bread under its arm streaked past them as fast as its short brown legs could carry it. A big man with a moustache, wearing an apron sprinted after the squirrel. He was dusted with flour, a floppy white hat on his head and a wooden rolling pin clenched in his hand.

"Stop thief!" the man shouted. He nearly knocked the three of them over as he bounded after the squirrel.

Chester stood for a moment transfixed, his jaw dropped, shocked. Then he turned and dashed after the baker and the squirrel. "Father!" he yelled.

Rubberface and Sam looked at each other. Rubberface jerked his head toward Chester. "Let's go." They ran to catch up with the squirrel.

The baker and Chester's father disappeared around a corner with Chester close behind. Sam zipped past the corner with Rubberface and saw the older squirrel crouched near a large water barrel. The baker stopped in the middle of the street and whacked the rolling pin in the flat of his hand, scanning the sidewalks and storefronts for the squirrel.

Chester darted among the people walking in the street and made his way toward his father. On the way, he scooted under a woman's long petticoat for cover. She screamed, jumped in the air and came down in a heap. She glared at him, picked up the umbrella, got to her feet and brushed the dust from her dress. "Rodent!" she snapped.

Chester bolted for his father who was still hiding behind the barrel. The woman chased after Chester and struck the ground trying to hit him. He dodged the blows and slipped past her.

The baker saw Chester's father peeking from behind the barrel and made for him.

A drainpipe attached to the building emptied into the rain barrel. Chester huddled with his father behind the barrel and pointed to it. Sam could see the two of them talking excitedly as the baker and woman approached. Chester, exasperated, gestured wildly to his father as they drew near. They stopped talking when the woman's umbrella thumped the rain barrel.

Chester and his father scampered to other side of the barrel, climbed to the lip of it over the water, and scaled the drainpipe. Chester first, his father bringing up the rear. When they neared the top by the roof, the baker hit the drainpipe with the rolling pin a good, solid thwack jolting the squirrels.

By now a crowd had formed. The woman waved the umbrella at Chester and shouted, "Come down you scoundrels!"

The older squirrel lost his footing and began to slide down the pipe toward the baker who banged it with his rolling pin. "Take the bread!" he yelled to Chester. Chester had made it to the top. He leaned over, extended his arm and reached for the bread. He got hold of it and started to pull. "Let go of it Dad," he shouted, "and grab the pipe."

"I can't," his father said, "hold on—"

Rubberface and Sam made it to the rain barrel. Sam looked up and realized the old squirrel's feet weren't in contact with the pipe. He was climbing up the loaf of bread toward his son. Chester hung over the side of the roof. His eyes wild and scared. "C'mon Pop, you can make it. I know you can."

"Barely," his father croaked. He was heavier than his son and out of breath.

The baker smacked the drainpipe a good one and it rattled all the way up. Chester's father lost control of the bread and hung on with just one hand. He clawed with the other to get a grip on the loaf. The woman brought her umbrella up under the older squirrel and poked him in the butt. He jerked up and put both paws on the bread. By now, Chester had the loaf teetering on the edge of the roof. It rocked back and forth like a crazy seesaw.

Sam glanced over and could scarcely believe his eyes. The baker put his foot on the lip of the rain barrel, grabbed hold of the shaky drainpipe and hoisted himself up. He stood on the barrel and teetered. He dropped the rolling pin on the ground and reached for the squirrel's tail swishing back and forth two feet above him.

There was a crack and the drainpipe fell away. Chester gave a mighty tug and catapulted his father onto the roof, bread and all.

The baker's eyes widened. He was suspended for a moment above the rain barrel. Then, he came down in a great splash, drenching the woman and splashing Rubberface, Sam and the people standing close by.

The baker sat in the barrel, soaked. His face red as an apple, eyes popping mad. The two squirrels peeked over the rooftop at him, giggled and disappeared with the bread.

Sam heard a creak, then another, then a loud crack. The barrel gave way. Its sides flattened out like wagon spokes. The baker crashed to the ground in a soggy heap. He sat for a moment dazed. His forearms were caked with white flour, his apron soaked and soiled. Then he jumped up and shook his fist at the rooftop where the squirrels had been. "I'll get you…you little varmints, if it's the last thing I do."

The woman glared at the baker with her hands on her hips. "Look what you've done to my dress. You've ruined it. Who's going to pay for this, I'd like to know?" She held up the hem of her dress. There were faint yellow flowers on it crisscrossed by sprays of tobacco-colored mud. Her mouth quivered as if she was about to burst into tears.

The baker looked at her. The air left his broad chest in a long sigh. He seemed to deflate before her eyes. "I dunno, ma'am. I'm awfully sorry about the dress."

11

Rubberface and Sam stood in the street. Rubberface shook his head. His jowls flapped from side to side. "Well, I'll be."

"Looks like he found his father," Sam said.

"True, true. Now we've got to find them. Could be anywhere. High or low. They're squirrels. Easy for them to hide, disappear. The little skunks. Where did they go?" He rubbed his chin. "Hmmm...we should split up. See if we can find them. Can't be too far."

"What about my father?"

"Right. I know you want to get to Belltown, but this'll only take a couple minutes."

"I don't know, I—"

"C'mon, give it a try. We'll split up and look for a bit. If we don't find 'em I'll show you the way to Belltown. How's that?"

"I guess so."

"We'll circle 'round and 'round looking at the rooftops but look low, too. Keep going out until we hit the edge of town. It's not too far. When you hit the edge, come on back, I'll wait for you here."

"OK."

Sam watched Rubberface's back as he walked off. He didn't know what to make of the man. He hadn't done anything wrong but Sam didn't trust him. Sam turned and walked in the opposite direction on the wood-planked sidewalk. He glanced in a large plate glass window with DENTIST in gold letters across the top of it. A worried-looking, bearded man sat in a heavy chair on a low platform. The dentist stood beside him. He was a thin, bald man with a wooden mallet in one hand and what looked like a chisel in the other.

A man walked by from the other direction. He glanced in the window, then at Sam and said "Ouch," as he passed.

Sam walked on, looking for Chester and his father. A man stood in front of a shop with his hands in his pockets. He wore an apron that had once been white. It was covered with smears and red stains. His hat was tall, black and ratty-looking. There were hooks above him along the top of the window of his shop. Some were empty, some held various cuts and chunks of meat.

There was a yard with carts and wagons of various shapes and sizes. A sign with peeling red letters advertised Pre-Owned Vehicles, All Kinds. You Want 'Em, We've Got 'Em.

As he plodded by the worn wagons and tired-looking carriages Sam muttered, "I'm feeling kind of pre-owned myself."

Sam looked up the sidewalk. A mother approached with her son walking by her side. The boy looked a few years younger than Sam. He had a smooth, oval face and chattered to his mother, grinning.

Sam remembered a time with his father before they left on their trip. They were getting ready for bed and had just finished brushing their teeth. Sam stared in the mirror, his Dad's reflection above him. He cupped his face in his hands and said, "I think I have the face of a ten year old."

His father smiled, and then turned more serious. "Why do you say that, Sam?"

"I see the kids in the third grade. Their voices are higher than mine. I just think I look older than they do."

"I see," his father said. Then he knelt behind Sam and hugged him from the back. "Now I get it."

Sam stood on the sidewalk and recalled his father's face hovering in the mirror behind him. Tears came to his eyes. He wiped them off with the back of his hand. After the woman passed by with her son Sam heard the boy say, "He was crying Mom—why?"

"I don't know," his mother replied. "Probably he was sad."

Sam walked past a hat shop with woolen caps, domed bonnets and tall stovepipes. Then Poor Richard's Dry Goods & Sundries. In the window there was a wooden rake, shovels and hammers. In the corner was a wooden rocking horse with a sign over it that said: *Build your own Rocking Horse. Everything you need in this handy-dandy*

do-it-yourself kit. Sam stopped for a moment and stared at it. He heard a faint scratching sound, then an urgent whisper. "Hey—Sam."

Sam scanned the door of the shop, the nearby street, and the boardwalk he'd just passed for the source of the sound.

"Pssst—down here," the voice said again.

Sam glanced down. It was Chester peering out from beneath the sidewalk planks. "Don't look at me," Chester said, his voice raspy. "Somebody might see us. Then we'll be cooked for sure."

"Just listen," Chester continued. "Go the same direction you've been walking on this street. Keep going 'til you hit the edge of town. We'll be right behind you, don't worry. Gotta lay low so nobody sees us. Got me?"

Sam stared at the street and tried not to look like he was listening to an anxious squirrel giving directions. "What about Rubberface?"

Chester was silent for a moment. Sam stole a glance at him.

"Don't look!" Chester said, his voice tight. "Listen, he's a big boy. He can look after himself. We gotta get outta this town safe and sound."

"He was going to show me the way to Belltown," Sam protested.

"Right. Listen Sam, I've got the map. *I'll* show you, OK? C'mon. Let's get moving before somebody spots us."

"OK." Sam set off down the sidewalk. He heard rustling and scampering behind him. He glanced over his shoulder when he crossed the street. The squirrels were close together, crouching low and darting between the wheels of wagons. Chester's father had the half-eaten loaf of bread tucked under his arm like it was a football and he was racing to an imaginary goal line.

When Sam reached the end of town Chester yelled behind him, "Keep going. Take that road that curves off to the left. Don't look back. We'll follow."

Sam looked up and saw a sign that read: Belltown—5 miles. He set off. After he'd walked a while he heard Chester's voice again, panting, "Hold up, willya? This tall grass is tough going."

Sam sat down in a grassy patch by the side of the road and waited.

Chester emerged from the grass with his father by his side. The older squirrel clutched what was left of the bread. He looked tired, haggard and out of breath. "Sam, this is my father, Emmett. Emmett Smally."

"Pleased to meet you," Sam said, extending his hand.

Emmett took hold of it and gave it a limp shake. "Didn't know if I could keep up with you young fella."

"What about Rubberface?" Sam asked. "I think he's going to be angry we didn't wait for him and—"

"Don't trust him," Chester cut in. He looked at his father.

Emmett nodded and said, "He's the kind of friend that might not *be* much of a friend."

"Well, he said he'd show me the way to Belltown," Sam said.

"You're on it," Chester replied. "We'll walk with you a while. My dad has a woman friend up this way. Name's Florence."

"Let's go to Belltown," Sam said, getting up. "I've got to find my dad."

Emmett looked at the ground, lost in thought. His shoulders all bunched up.

"You OK, Dad?" Chester asked.

Emmett didn't look at his son. He nodded.

"Let's go then," Chester said, slapping his father on the back. "Boy it's good to see you again. Did I tell you I missed you?"

"About a dozen times," Emmett said, squinting straight ahead. "About a dozen times."

12

The three pilgrims walked on the rutted dirt road toward Belltown. Chester peppered his father with questions. Where had he been? Why didn't he write? Was there really a robbery? Did he steal a fortune in pirate gold and jewels? How 'bout it? Was he still on the run from the law?

Emmett looked over his shoulder as if he expected someone to come from behind, arrest him and haul him away. "I…I've been hiding out, son."

"Don't I *know* it," Chester snapped, losing patience. "C'mon Dad. What's with all your secrets anyway? Sam isn't going to turn you in, are you?"

Sam shook his head.

"See? Out with it, or *I'll* turn you in," Chester said.

"You wouldn't turn you poor old father in, would you?" Emmett said, his eyes moist.

"I might if he doesn't start talking. I been trying to find you Dad. And now that I have, what've I got? This…this…empty bucket?" He laughed a dry, hollow laugh.

"You *mean* it boy, don't you?" Emmett replied.

Chester gave his father a piercing look. "Darn right. Go on, Pop."

"Well...I...*we* did it. Me, Freddy Skeen and Archie Bellknap. Freddy's a packrat and Archie...he's a porcupine. Pretty ornery, but he gets the job done when you need a little muscle. We planned the whole thing out. 'Course *I* was the brains of the operation. That was one sweet deal. Stole it from a king west of here last name of Ferdinand. We were trying to rob from the rich and give to the poor. We weren't just selfish little—"

Chester chimed in and sang along, clapping his hands together. "When you've got a feeling, to do a little stealing—I guess any excuse will do."

Emmett glared back. "As I was saying...that king made his money off the backs of hard-working peasants. Had a lot more than he needed and we had a whole lot less than we wanted. Shoot, he probably stole it all anyway, that old weasel. Robbed some pirates of their booty. He was pirate too—a *land* pirate."

"How did you do it?" Sam asked. He wanted to believe Emmett, but he wasn't sure if the old squirrel was just making it up as he went along.

"I'm getting to that," Emmett replied. "It was a night without stars, overcast and black. Freddy—he did the digging. Burrowed right under the castle wall. He's got a brain the size of a peanut but I tell you, that rat can *dig*. We came out in a hallway not sure where we were. Had to get my bearings. Then we heard footsteps. Slipped into a wine cellar to hide out from the guards. Those boys had long swords. If they found us, they'd have run us through. Made hash of us."

"What then?" Chester asked.

"I was a little dizzy coming out of that cellar—fumes it was. Felt like I'd drunk a bottle of wine. Archie bumped into the wall. Would've been funny if we weren't so scared. We didn't know which door held the treasure. 'Course they were all locked. The king might be a nasty rogue, but he's no fool. Finally found the one, least I *thought* it was the one."

"How did you know?" Sam asked.

"I've got a nose for gold," Emmett said, sticking his chest out, cocking his head.

Chester burst out laughing and nudged Sam. "They call him Old Gold Nose."

Emmett suddenly stopped walking and stared at his son. "I expect a little respect from you. Father tries to do right by his son, put away some money for his boy and *this* is the thanks I get."

"Thanks? —my *foot*," Chester shot back. "You left me and Ma and Roscoe high and dry. Thank goodness Ma left us some food 'fore she died. *She's* the one took care of us."

Emmett held his tongue, nodded and started walking again more briskly than before. "Humph. Like I said, I've got a nose for gold. I stood before that door trembling. Could almost smell the doubloons, rubies, sapphires. My whiskers were twitching. I told 'em, 'Here boys, this is the one. I swear on my grandmother's grave.' There was a little crack at the bottom of the door. I said, 'Work on it Freddy, use your teeth, your jaws. Go ahead man—*gnaw*.' He looked at me like I was nuts but gave it a go. Archie and I kept watch in case those guards came back. Actually, they did come back. I was sweating, thought we were finished. But they ducked into the wine cellar, sat down and had themselves a merry old time."

"Was it the right door?" Sam asked.

Emmett smiled. "Freddy gnawed at the wood quiet as he could with the guards down the hall. He peeked through the hole and whispered, 'I see it. There's a chest in there.' He made a big enough hole and went in. Unlocked the door and opened it. We were in like a breeze. Crept over to the chest. My heart was thumping like a big bass drum. The sky had cleared and the moon was full, shining on it from a high window. It was something. As long as I live I'll never—"

"Was it the treasure?" Chester broke in.

"Was it *ever*," Emmett replied, proudly. "Not even a lock on it. Guess he never figured anybody'd get that far. Freddy pulled back the top and there it was. Glory be! Doubloons. Rubies the size of cherries. Sapphires big as grapes. And diamonds. Boys, let me tell you. I thought I was sitting at the King's table with the heavenly hosts. Riches untold. Nothing you'll ever see will get your heart pumping quite like the—"

"What then?" Sam interrupted. He felt they were moving slowly and wanted to get to the next town. The old squirrel seemed to be poking along.

"Well, we were dazzled. Giggling like schoolboys. Freddy wanted to sit right down and count it. Crazy Archie wanted to jump in the chest and roll around in it. The guy was batty. I said, 'Boys, we've got to get this thing outta here right now. Lift it, don't drag it.' 'Course nobody wants to leave it behind after we did all that hard work."

"An *honest* living," Chester piped in.

Emmett fixed his son with a look. "We could barely lift it. I saw some kind of animal skin on a chair, disgusting thing really, like it was once one of us, skin off my back. But time was of the essence as the poets say. I put it on the floor and the three of us raised the chest and set it down on the pelt. The thing weighed about a million pounds. Then we grabbed hold of the handles. I pushed, Freddy and Archie pulled. We got it movin', smooth as you please."

"What about the guards?" Sam asked.

"They were drinking. We could hear them down the hall in the wine cellar, carrying on. Even started singing. Some song about pirates and a dead man's chest. We were scared they'd find us. I was glad they were singing. We got the chest down the hall and found the hole we'd come in. Then I knew we had a problem—a *big* one."

"What?" Chester said, his tone insistent.

Emmett shook his head. "The hole was too small. We could've tried some other doors and taken our chances but we voted. Freddy digs, or we try the doors. See if we can't find a way out of the castle."

"What did you do?"

"We were split down the middle. I voted Freddy dig. Archie said try the doors. Freddy was undecided. I said, 'OK, Freddy start digging, I'll stay here with you. And Archie, you try some doors, find a way out.'"

Sam nodded. Chester shook his head and patted his foot, impatient with his father.

"I'm standing by Freddy, guarding the loot and he's digging like a hound dog. Archie's workin' the doors. They're all locked. He turns down the hall so I can't see him anymore. Then I hear a shriek. He opened the door to somebody's bed chamber, one of the maids I guess. He tears back down the hall to us. Freddy's digging furiously now. The guards are shouting, stumbling. They're talking to the woman that screamed. Then I hear heavy footsteps coming for us."

"Yikes," Sam said.

"Freddy and Archie jump in the hole and pull on the chest with everything they've got. I'm pushing and it's going in. About halfway in it's stuck, won't budge. I hear them behind me and turn. It's two guards, their swords out, comin' straight for me. 'Push!' I yell to the boys. But they don't, they're still pulling the thing. The guards are ten feet away now. Then I yank it with all my might. Chest comes flying out of the hole and nearly lands on top of me. I duck and it hits the ground. Top cracks open and a couple doubloons pop out. Rolling right toward the guards. They stop, nearly crash into one another and reach down and pick 'em up. Can you believe it? I figured that was my cue. I dove in the hole, crawled through, and high-tailed it out of there. I took one look back. The hole was too small for the guards to follow. I saw a sword stabbing at the opening. Scared me to death. That could've been *me*."

"Don't tell me," Chester said.

"What?" Emmett answered, rattled.

"The gold," Chester said. "You didn't get any. Left it all behind, Mr. Gold Nose?"

"There's no need for impudence, son," Emmett said. "We were lucky to get out of there with our lives. Another moment or two with those guards and it would have been dear-old-dad-may-he-rest-in-peace." He pulled his paw across his neck like he was cutting his own throat.

Chester winced.

"That's it up ahead," Emmett said, "Florence's place. Lives halfway up that tree in a hollow. That's good news 'cause I'm feeling a little dusty with all this yakkin' I've been doin'. I could use a drink. Not that it hasn't been a fine trip, boys. Chances are, Florence is home. She don't get out too often."

Sam looked at the giant oak in the distance. He knew Emmett was excited to be back with Florence and Chester was happy to be reunited with his father, but Belltown was still a ways off. It tugged at him to be on *his* way.

13

The travelers stood at the base of the tree and stared up the trunk through the thick, twisting limbs. Emmett yelled several times. A squirrel popped out of a hole halfway up the trunk.

"Hello Darlin'," Emmett shouted. "Brought a friend and my... my boy, Chester. This other boy, he's OK, name's Sam. It's been an adventure—"

"You got anything?" Florence yelled, her voice sharp and raspy.

"Just a crust of bread, my love. And I nearly got killed getting it." Emmett held up the remainder of the loaf.

Florence crossed her arms, glared at him and snapped, "Last of the big-time providers, that's you."

"We'll be up in a minute, sweets. I've already eaten, so this is for you."

He held up the stump of bread as if it was a gift from another world. Florence shook her head and ducked inside the tree.

Chester elbowed his father. "What about Sam? He can't come up unless he's good at tree climbing."

His father had been staring at Florence, a worried look on his face. "Right, would you like—"

"I've got to go," Sam cut in. "Looks like you've got some catching up to do. I'll be fine, don't worry about me."

"I guess this is goodbye then," Chester said, his eyes moist. "All you do is stay on this road. It'll take you right to Belltown. I'd go, but—" He nodded toward his father.

Sam was feeling a little sad. Tired of goodbyes. Before he let it get to him he shook their hands and said, "So long. Maybe I'll catch up with you some other time."

Emmett turned and began climbing the tree. He was clumsy, balancing the crust of bread on his shoulder.

"OK," Chester said to Sam's back. "I'll see you then." He nodded and followed his father up the great black trunk.

Sam walked briskly away. It seemed like it was taking forever to get to Belltown. His father was probably half crazy by now wondering what had become of him. Got to keep moving, he told himself. He passed low hills covered in tall grass dotted with occasional maples and firs. There was a good-sized grey hawk circling overhead. Probably looking for field mice, Sam guessed.

That's it! He thought. Why not be a hawk for a short while? I'll get to Belltown a heckuva lot faster than plodding this dusty road.

Sam stopped, looked up and trained his eyes on the bird. He became slightly dizzy, breathing slower, as it made loose circles in the sky. Then Sam *was* the bird, lifted on invisible breezes, the wind holding him up like an unseen hand above the grassy field. He could see butterflies below him, even insects in the grass. He saw the silver glint of a stream up ahead and the roofs of fallen-down farmhouses.

He heard things. Rustlings. Bees humming beneath him. He couldn't understand their language but he knew they were talking.

He tried his wings and flew straight up. The breezes rocked him back and forth. Gotta learn how to do this a little better, he told himself. Steer, Sam, steer. He made a wide arc and then figure eights. He could see the rooftops of Five Corners in the distance and the large oak where Florence lived.

He turned and let the wind carry him toward Belltown. Now he was really moving. No more of this crawling down the road like a slug. Sure beats walking, he thought. He laughed, surprised at the sharpness of the sound he made.

He heard loud whacks and an odd ringing sound behind him. That's weird, he thought, doesn't seem like that sound belongs in these fields and meadows. There were voices mixed in with the sounds. Worried voices. He couldn't make out the words but the feeling was of someone in danger. I've got to keep going, he told himself. Then he heard a deeper voice, a man. He couldn't place it at first, then it came to him—Rubberface!

He wheeled around and zoomed back the way he'd come. As he approached the huge oak he could see it was Rubberface. He was chopping furiously at the tree with a double-bladed axe, cursing under his breath.

Sam circled overhead as Rubberface shouted up the tree. "I know you've got it, you old coot. Throw the treasure down and I'll stop chopping. *All* of it, jewels, doubloons—everything."

"I don't have it, I swear," Emmett protested. He held on to a large limb. The tree had begun to sway.

"You're lying," Rubberface yelled. "You left me in town. Thought you could ditch me, did you? What do I look like, a fool?"

"You don't just look like one, you *are* one." Chester chanted, "Rubberface, Rubberface, fell from grace, right on his face. The man ain't nothin' but a big disgrace. Rubberface, Rubberface…."

"Taunt me will you?" Rubberface shouted. "You'll be sorry you ever double-crossed me. I tried to be friends with you."

"Some friend *you* turned out to be," Chester shot back.

Florence wrung her hands and moaned. "This is my home. What's to become of it? He's chopping it down. Emmett, for heavensakes *do* something."

Emmett shrugged. "Yes dear, I know. What do you want me to do? He's got an axe and there's only one way down."

"It's your fault he's here," she wailed. "I should have never let you come back. That's the thanks I get. I'll be ruined. My things...."

Chester darted inside and came out with his arms filled with acorns. He chucked them at Rubberface but missed. It seemed to infuriate the man even more.

"What're you doing?" Florence shrieked at Chester. "That's my winter food supply, young man." She turned to Emmett. "You show up with your long lost son and *this* happens. It's outrageous. I never—"

There was a loud CRACK! Florence stopped in mid-sentence, her eyes wide and frightened.

"No, no, my things, my dishes," Florence gasped. "My antiques."

"Forget your antiques," Emmett said. "Think of your neck."

Sam circled lower, swooped in through the leaves and landed on a branch a few feet from the frightened squirrels. Rubberface didn't notice, concentrating on his chopping.

There came a splitting sound from down below. Then another.

Emmett was terrified. He held up his hands, stepped back and nearly slipped off the branch. "Well, I guess this is it. If the fall doesn't kill us, we'll be crushed to death by the claws of this, this, scary-lookin' hawk. I guess it don't matter once you're gone. One way is as good as another if you—"

Chester cut in, "Dad, grab some acorns! Defend yourself."

"Defend our home," Florence pleaded.

"Wait," Sam said, "It's me—Sam."

The squirrels froze as if they were put on pause by some magic button. No one flinched or moved a muscle.

"S-s-s-sam?" Chester stammered. "Is that you—how on earth?"

"I can become things," Sam answered. "I've had a special power ever since I came to this world. I became a hawk. You don't have to worry I'll eat you. I heard the axe and came back to help."

"What'll we do?" Emmett said, his eyes shiny with concern.

Chester came closer and studied Sam. "Nice beak. Sharp eyes, too."

"I don't see so great up close," Sam said, "but distance? All I can say is...*wow*. I've got an idea. Hop on my back and I'll take you down to the ground one by one."

"We're not too heavy?" Florence asked.

"Don't know," Sam said. "Won't know 'til we try." He heard another whack from below. "No time to waste." He turned to Florence. "How about you first?"

Florence looked to the squirrels as if she needed approval.

The tree shook. "Hah!" Rubberface shouted. He paused, stared at his handiwork for a moment and then picked up the axe and worked with a fury. "Won't be long now."

"Go," Emmett said to Florence. "Go now."

She approached Sam and climbed on his back. "Easy with the claws," he said, and then, "that's better." When she was secure, Sam edged down the branch, sagging a little under her weight. "OK, here goes."

He lifted off, wobbled slightly, then flapped his wings and righted himself. They swooped down, coasted to a stop and she climbed off. He immediately flew back up for Chester and Emmett.

"Who's next?" Sam said.

"You Dad," Chester said.

Emmett struck a noble pose as if he was getting ready to make a brief, important speech. "Now son, I—"

There was a crack from the base of the tree. The limbs and leaves shuddered.

"Go on, son!" Emmett yelled, looking down at the top of Rubberface's head.

Rubberface stopped and shouted up through the branches. "I gave you a chance to come clean with me and share the riches, but would you? Absolutely not. You'll be sorry when—" Then he stared, astonished, as Chester climbed on Sam's back and Sam took off. "What the? You good-for-nothing cowards."

Sam swooped low and brought Chester down beside Florence.

"That was fun," Chester said, getting off. "Let's do it again."

Sam gave him a look.

"Sorry," Chester said.

Sam flew back to the branch. Emmett was shaking with fear, clutching the crust of bread he'd brought with him on their journey.

"Why don't you just leave that?" Sam said, impatiently.

"Couldn't." Emmett looked like he was being asked to leave something priceless. "We'll need to eat, you know."

The tree began to sway back and forth. There was a snap, then a series of splitting, tearing sounds.

"Get on," Sam said, "now!"

Emmett climbed on Sam's back with the bread beneath his arm. On the way down he lost control of the bread as it tumbled to the grass and nearly slipped off Sam's back trying to catch it.

Sam landed with a soft thump. Emmett leapt off his back and ran toward the tree and the small loaf lying in the grass.

"Pop—don't!" Chester yelled.

"Damn rodents," Rubberface bellowed. He dropped his axe and ran toward Emmett who was bending over the bread.

Emmett grabbed the bread, glanced at Rubberface charging toward him and ran.

There was a thunderous CRACK behind Rubberface. The tree came toward them. Florence, Chester and Sam stepped back as it crashed to the ground. A great mass of leaves and limbs quivered on the ground in front of them. Then they stopped. It was quiet. Rubberface and Emmett were nowhere in sight.

Chester ran frantically from limb to limb peering beneath clumps of leaves shouting, "Father, where are you? Answer me Dad!"

Sam looked at his wings and thought *uh-oh, I'd better be getting back to Sam.* He closed his eyes for a moment and remembered his father and mother. Pictured them in the kitchen of their old house. One of the few happy memories he had of them together. His father was making blueberry pancakes, Sam's favorite. His mother sat at the table cradling a cup of coffee in her hands. "It warms them, Sam," she said when he asked why she did it. Then she took his hand and placed his palm on her cup, "See?"

Sam breathed with the memory and let it go through his body like blood. He felt his arms and legs growing, rising quickly, his bones heavier than when he was a hawk. He was returning, coming back. His hearing changed and became less intense, precise. Then, he was Sam again. He opened his eyes and saw Chester scurrying from branch to branch. Florence had joined the search, stepping over twigs and lifting up leaves.

"I found him," Chester shouted. "Over here, come quick!"

Florence and Sam stepped over fallen branches to where Chester stood.

There was Emmett, flat on his back. Chester knelt by his side and listened to his heart. He picked up Emmett's paw, dropped it and crouched by his nose. Chester looked up at Sam. "He's still breathing. I think I can hear a thin whistle from old Gold Nose."

Emmett blinked, turned his head and looked at his son. "Ouch," he said.

"What happened?" Chester asked.

"I was in the air—then…flat on my back," the older squirrel said. "Tree must have thrown me." He felt his head. "Don't remember much. Got a big bump here. Think I might've hit my head. Maybe I've got a percussion," he added, thoughtfully. He pulled himself up to a sitting position and frowned.

Chester laughed and slapped his hand on the ground. "Concussion, Dad, *con*cussion. Unless you mean the tree was beating on your head like a drum."

Emmett winced. "That's what it *felt* like." He noticed the crust of bread lying a few feet away. "Safe. Now there's a miracle for you. At least we won't go hungry."

"That's all you care about," Florence sniffed. She crossed her arms and patted her feet on the ground impatiently.

"What about Rubberface, anybody see where he went?" Emmett asked.

"Could be anywhere," Sam replied, stepping over the limbs and searching. "Guy's got an axe. Probably still dangerous."

Sam climbed over the big tree trunk and yelled. "I found the axe!"

The squirrels scampered over except Emmett. He hobbled, using the bread as a makeshift crutch.

"Oh no," Sam said. He knelt down by the thick trunk. "It's him." The squirrels gathered 'round. The only parts of Rubberface that were visible were his frayed pant legs and the curious shoes he wore.

"Change his name to pancake," Chester said.

No one laughed.

"Much as I didn't like the man, I hate to see him end up like this," Emmett replied.

"Humph," Florence added. She spit into the grass. "My house is ruined. My priceless antiques—poof!" She held up her hands, looked at the sky and sighed.

"He won't have to worry about money or anything else now," Sam said, nodding to Rubberface lying beneath the tree. He got up slowly and looked at Emmett. "I have to go. Are you gonna be OK?"

"Well I..." Emmett looked like he was going to give a speech, glanced at Chester and stopped. "...Think I'll be all right." He rubbed the bump on the back of his head.

Sam shook hands all around, turned, and took off down the road toward Belltown before he could think about Rubberface, why he tried to chop the squirrels down, the friends he was leaving and how far he still had to go to find his father.

14

I gotta shake the dust off," Sam said to no one. "Feels like I've been going forever and not getting anywhere."

He looked up the road. Heat waves shimmered over the dusty surface. He'd seen Belltown before from the air. He had no idea how far it was as he plodded along. He saw an apple tree up ahead and made for it. He stood in the cool shade beneath it and rested his elbow on the split-rail fence that ran along the field. He looked back and saw the enormous downed oak. He imagined the squirrels talking, arguing, trying to figure out what to do next.

A robin landed on the fence ten feet from him. It cocked its head and studied Sam as if *he'd* just landed from the sky.

Sam gazed at the bird. Sure would make the miles fly by, he thought. Can't be that far to Belltown but this is taking forever.

He felt the rise and fall of his breath as he looked at the bird. He noticed its shiny black eyes and the tiny jerks of its head. Then, almost as if it was calling, "Here I am," Sam *was* the robin, perched on the splintery wooden rail. He looked over and held out a wing, studied the way it fanned out, everything there, nothing missing. Sound as can be. His orange breast was rising and falling. He leapt from the fence and flapped his wings. Aha! Magic. Air beneath him. He was flying. It took more work to get up above the trees than when he was a hawk but he was doing it. Nothing but his thoughts to hold him to the earth. "Why not," he chirped, "this is fun!" When he spoke it sounded like soft clucking.

Sam flew higher and higher. He'd been up in a plane a few times, astonished at the mountains below him. The snow-capped peaks, silvery rivers and shadowy valleys. This was different. He wasn't in a plane, *he* was the plane. Coasting, zooming, soaring—flying! Yes, yes, yes, yahoo!

He saw a man on a horse beneath him plodding along, plowing a field. Stacks of hay like peculiar tufted straw hats. Cows grazing and the rough shake tops of barns and houses. The way the road curved. He heard birds talking to one another. Snatches of conversations about nesting sites, places to raise kids, good hunting and fishing spots. Even an argument between two crows. The wife scolding the husband for staying out too late with his friends. The husband shouting back, "How *dare* you accuse me!"

Sam wanted to linger, hear the whole conversation, but he was on his way. He saw a clump of buildings ahead rippling in the heat. The rooftops of Belltown.

He decided he'd better come in for a landing before he got to town and walk the last stretch of road. No telling who would see him and what they'd make of his changing back into Sam before their eyes.

As he got closer he saw a small grove of trees and swooped down, landing in the middle of a cherry tree. What luck! He was thirsty and the cherries were plump and ripe. He gulped a few down and spit out the pits. How refreshing. The juice burst in his beak like sweet music. "Ahhh," he said.

"Ahem," came a low, raspy voice behind him.

Sam turned. There was an old black crow on a branch a few feet from him, its wings dusty and frayed. The crow scowled and spat a cherry pit at Sam. It bounced off his breast.

"Just what do you think you're doing?" the crow asked.

"What's it look like?" Sam said, a little put out. "Same as you. It's a hot day and I'm thirsty."

"Get your own tree then," the crow snapped. "This one's mine."

Before Sam could reply, the crow hopped closer and spat another pit. It hit Sam on the side of his beak.

"Hey!" Sam yelled. "No need for that. Plenty of cherries in this tree." He backed away from the crow. "There's no reason we can't share."

"I'll give you a reason," the crow said. He jumped, landed on the branch in front of Sam, raised his wing and clipped Sam across the beak.

Sam fell back and the crow kept coming, pecking at his feet.

Sam lost his footing on the branch and stumbled backward. He tripped on a twig and went down, spinning beak over tail. He landed in the dry dusty grass with a thump, got up and shook his head.

The crow swooped down and pecked him again. This time a glancing blow that narrowly missed his eye. "When I tell you to git, I mean *GIT!*" He beat Sam about the head with his big black wings.

Sam covered his head and fell in the dust. *I've got to get back up,* he thought. *Remember, Sam, remember,* he told himself. *Breathe. Come on back.* The crow was kicking him now with his hard, scaly feet. Sam felt a sharp pain in his legs and back.

Then he was breathing and remembering. Letting the air out of his lungs and recalling when he was a little guy and a bigger kid with spiky, black hair had pushed him off his wagon and grabbed the handle. "Gimme that—I want it!" he yelled at Sam and started walking off with it. Sam came up behind the bigger boy and yanked his shoulder back with his hand. The kid dropped the wagon handle grip. Sam picked it up, looked him in the eye and said, "Go ahead, make a move. We'll see what's what." To Sam's surprise the kid backed away.

Sam got up and pecked the crow's breast. The bigger bird was stunned and retreated a few steps. "Oh—so you're gonna fight are you? I'll show you...."

He came at Sam again. His eyes were black and shiny as polished marbles.

Sam stood his ground. His chest rose and fell. His heart thumped like a stick on a tight drumhead. "OK," he said, letting the air out of his lungs. "If you want me, you can have me. But you're gonna have to take *all* of me." With that he felt his body expand and rise. His chest filled like a balloon. His wings disappeared and became heavy with flesh and bones. His shoulders filled out and his beak vanished. His legs were scratched and smarting, his nose wet. He wiped it with the back of his hand and saw blood.

Sam towered over the astonished crow who retreated and tripped, falling on his tail. Sam reached down and grabbed the terrified bird. "Pick on a little guy, willya?"

The crow jerked in his hand like a wind-up toy. "Sorry...little fella...I mean sir. I never meant any harm. Just wanted some cherries, you understand. Don't kill me, I'm just a poor—"

"You're a poor excuse for a crow, that's what you are."

Sam walked out from beneath the tree into the sunlight gripping the bird. "I could squeeze the stuffing outta you but I'm not going to. If I ever come back this way and find out you've been mistreating somebody smaller than you you're gonna pay a price. Understand?"

The crow nodded. "Yes, of course I—"

"A *high* price," Sam snapped, staring at the crow's beady eyes.

"I'll behave," the crow croaked, looking at the ground.

"Be off with you then." Sam gave the bird one last squeeze and threw it up in the air as high as he could.

The crow tumbled and started to fall. Then it regained its wings and flapped in circles above Sam's head. "You'll be sorry you ever laid a hand on me. You little—"

Sam picked up a rock from the road, tossed it up and caught it in his hand.

The crow took off toward Belltown without another word.

15

Sam helped himself to more cherries until he had his fill. He scanned the sky to see if the crow would come back to bother him. It didn't.

The closer he got to Belltown, the busier and noisier the road became. Carts thumped by. Horses clip-clopped on the road, pulling carriages.

He saw black people, brown people, white people. Women with feathers in their hats and long flowing skirts. A man with a dusty leather cap and dirty red scarf around his neck.

A boy a few years older than Sam drove a herd of goats toward town. He was nut-brown, ragged and barefoot. He brandished a stick and yelled their names to keep them from straying into the tall grass by the side of the road. "Victor, Neely, Carson, come back here! Tessie, Flora, Dora, Lonnie, Peaches, Maisy—where are you going?" His voice was hoarse from shouting.

Maisy. Sam smiled. "That's the name of my Gameboy electronic dog. Well I'll be doggoned," he said softly and laughed to himself.

As the boy passed, Sam almost said something about his dog Maisy but decided the boy wouldn't know what he was talking about.

Sam fell in behind some circus folk. There were monkeys with bright red and yellow hats riding on the back of wolf-like dogs the size of ponies.

Two clowns with huge shoes and enormous pants walked side by side. The man's hair was an orange ball of frizz and the woman's was tied up in strange-looking green and black coils.

Sam stopped and stared at her hair, transfixed. It swayed back and forth. A tongue flicked out the knob at the top. She had a snake on her head!

A short, stout juggler casually flipped balls over his head and around his back. He was a goat-headed man with short horns and yellow eyes. His partner had the body of a tall, slim woman with the head of a giraffe. She caught the balls seemingly without looking and tossed them back to the goat-man. There were five balls in the air. They didn't stop and didn't miss a beat.

A woman in a beautiful green silk robe was next. She had the head of a lioness and carried an umbrella to shield her from the sun. Behind her were four monkeys, two on each side in matching pale-green vests. They held up the train of her long robe so it wouldn't drag in the dust, kept their heads high, concentrated, and barely seemed to notice the people they passed.

Then came the carts: brightly painted, red, yellow and blue. A man with a top hat and dusty tails led the way. He had a black mustache curled up at the ends and sat atop a wagon with the name of the circus painted on the side of it. He held a megaphone to his mouth and barked:

"Alexander T. Farnsworth's most Unbelievable Show of Shows. The greatest circus the world has ever seen. Come young, come old. Don't miss out or you'll be sorry you did. The biggest, brightest, bestest, whether you're north, south, east or westest. Remember...if it's excitement, thrills, chills, somersaults, dangerous tricks, impossible escapes, wild animals and juggling—this is the show to get up and go to. And clowns—did I forget to mention clowns? They'll make your sides ache with laughter and your heart jump out of your chest with joy. Don't miss it—this is it! The one. The only. The circus you've got to see before you die.

"Brought to you by: Hapsburg's House of Hair. If it's barbering you need, come on down to Hapsburg's. It doesn't matter if you're young or old, fat or thin. They've got shaves—from the cradle to the grave, cuts, waves, tints, you want em, we've got em. Bald? Not a problem, Hapsburg's has wigs of every shape and size. No head too big, no dome too small.

"Also sponsored by: Bleckman's Fire-Proof Paint. Yes friends, for the paint that resists any and all campfires, bonfires, flames, flare-ups and conflagrations, candles, combustion and sparks in the dark —it's Bleckman's. Comes in all shades of grey, blue and brown and of course the ever popular white.

"And don't forget Tuttles Printing and Bookbinding. If it's rip-snorting tales of knights, round tables, swordplay and chivalry—Tuttles is the place to go. And romance, do they have romance? I'll say. Why, boy meets girl, frog meets toad, spider meets fly. You'll meet sweet-cheeked heroines and broad-chested heroes. Read about dangerous scrapes and dragons in castles. Stories that will make you howl with laughter, weep with joy and shiver in the middle of the night. You'll find it all here under one roof. Don't be down at the heels, out of sorts, lonesome and heartbroken. Pick up a good book. They'll always keep you company and never let you down as long as you...."

The man with the mustache rolled out of range until Sam couldn't hear him anymore. He shook his head and laughed. Next was a huge bear on a tiny bicycle with a serious expression on his face. He wore a small conical red hat and a purple vest with blue trim. His coat was dark and glossy. The bear made precise figure eights behind the yellow cart.

Sam dropped his jaw and stared in disbelief. "The poster! It's the bear from the poster—the one in the farmhouse—come to life!" He said it aloud, looked around to nudge someone, tell them his amazing discovery, but there was no one to share it with.

The bear on the bicycle rolled away, staring at his feet on the pedals, paying no attention to Sam.

Then came two more bears, male and female, Sam guessed. They faced one another, with one arm around their partner and another held aloft. They were waltzing. The male bear seemed to be counting under his breath and concentrating on his steps. The female wore a purple skirt, held her head up high and smiled broadly.

Next was a large cart led by a team of four horses. On top of it in tiers was an incredible collection of musicians in a wild assortment of uniforms. A bespectacled monkey tooted on a clarinet, his brows furrowed, concentrating. He sat next to a Panda bear with a dreamy look in its eyes. It stroked a harp, looking off in the distance. Next to the bear an otter stood on a low riser in a frayed blue band uniform with a pair of small cymbals in its hands. It clapped them together willy-nilly without regard for the beats the orchestra made. Beside the otter was a donkey-headed man. He wore a rust-colored jacket with yellow trim and dull, brown, mismatched pants. He looked with disgust at the otter's musicianship and strummed the guitar in his lap so softly Sam could barely hear it.

In front of the donkey fellow was a creature with the head of a fox and the body of a man in a spotless red band uniform. He raised a trumpet to his lips and blew a string of notes like a golden stepladder, high, bright and brassy. When finished, he pulled a white handkerchief from his jacket pocket and dabbed at his forehead. Beside the fox sat a curious being. A woman, Sam guessed, with a purple dress. She had long, dark hair on top of her head in a series of rope-like coils. At the very top of her hair was a large white flower. She had a full black beard, dark eyebrows and a frowning expression. The woman picked up the trombone in her lap and blew several long rhythmic blats. A gorilla stood beside her, grinned and pounded a big bass drum with a mallet. It swung its body in time with the beat. In front of the gorilla was stick-thin man with the head of a stork. His fingers flew over the piccolo perched at the end of his beak. Beside him sat a heavyset turtle in a faded green uniform who bobbed his head to the music and honked train-whistle blasts on the harmonica.

Sam was amazed. The music they made was a bewildering stew of styles that still managed to sound like music. It teetered on the verge of collapse and then veered back to some kind of song unlike anything he'd ever heard. His jaw dropped open in wonder. He stood stock-still by the side of the road. Nothing in his piano practice and playing had prepared him for *this* kind of music, whatever it was. The music sprayed off the groaning cart like a wild garden hose throbbing, unwinding and drenching everyone nearby with its great lumpy squall.

He was staring at the procession in happy bewilderment when a man approached and stood before him. He was short, not much taller than Sam. He wore a top hat, black tuxedo jacket and pants with frayed cuffs. His white shirt was worn and stained, shoes dusty and black. His face was small, lined and precise, with a salt and pepper goatee and dark eyes set back in his head. He smiled and showed Sam the gap in his front teeth.

"Osmo's the name," he said, still smiling, "short for Os Mosis In Excelsius Dayos. Magic is my business. My motto? 'If it's not magic, it's not worth it.' You're better off laying bricks for a living. What's your name young fella?"

"Sam," he answered, watching the musical cart creak down the road. Its wild sounds grew softer as it rolled away.

Osmo swung his arm from behind his back and startled Sam. In his hand was a great fan of cards.

"Don't worry," Osmo said, "it's only cards. Pick a card, any card. Go ahead, take one. Don't show me, let me guess."

Sam pulled a card from the deck and glanced at it.

"Ace of Spades," Osmo proclaimed. "Am I right or am I right?"

Sam nodded.

"Of course it means something," Osmo continued, "they *all* mean something."

"What?"

"Pick another card and I'll tell yah." Osmo held the cards before Sam, waiting.

"OK." Sam picked another card and held it to his chest.

"King of Hearts, sonny boy."

Sam grinned and shook his head. "How in the heck do you—"

"I know, I know—boy do I know," Osmo said, laughing. "Ace of Spades not so good. Dark forces at work there, m'boy. Steer clear of anybody with one of those, y'hear?" He stared at the ground, a serious look on his face. "Long journey, Sam. That's what you're on. You want to get back to something or someone you've lost along the way. Ace of spades means you might have trouble getting there." He looked in Sam's astonished eyes and then back at the ground. "Umhmm, I could tell you it's a long journey, but heck, they all say that. 'Course in this case it's true. The journey doesn't take much time but it *seems* long. You're missing someone—your mother or your father." He looked up.

Sam nodded, his cheeks flushed. He felt like he might begin to cry, set his mouth firm and looked off in the distance. "That's right, I've been trying to find—"

"Well...I don't know much," Osmo said, plucking the Ace of Spades from Sam's hand. "This one spells trouble, but the King of Hearts is a good sign. Means you could be on your way."

"Do you have any idea where I might find my father?"

"I'm not from around here," Osmo said, "but you could try Belltown, it's as good a place as any. I'm part of the circus as you might have guessed. I've got to be on my way or they'll get started without me. Can't have that. Might figure out they don't need me. Come see us if you can. Keep the King of Hearts, might bring you luck. We could all use a little luck from time to time. 'Sides, if you come to see the show, that card will get you in free. Show it to 'em at the door. Save your money for more important things, like eating."

With that, Osmo bowed to Sam and tipped his hat. "Goodbye, I've really got to be going. Cheer up. You'll find your father I have a feeling," he tapped his breast, "right *here*."

"So long," Sam said, clutching the card as the curious man turned and ran after the departing circus caravan.

16

Sam stood for a moment and watched the man run down the street after the circus. Puffs of dust rose from his feet like smoke.

He let the air out of his lungs in a long, sad sigh. His heart ached. He missed his father and mother. He'd made a Father's Day card for his dad before they left on their vacation. It said:

Happy Father's Day
I used to eat baby food
But now I eat salmon
I used to be free
But now I'm stuck in school
I used to love my parents
But now I love them even more
Love, Sam

He looked at the departing circus, people coming and going on the road, horses clopping in the dust and heat and wished for a moment he was back in school. Back where he *knew* things. Facts. Figures. What they would have for lunch, even. It was written on the blackboard every day. The answers to long division and multiplication questions. When the bell would ring for recess and the end of the day. Looking forward to teaching his digital dog Maisy new tricks on his Gameboy in the big yellow bus on the way home after school. Telling fart jokes with his best friend Jeffrey in back. Laughing, wrestling, fooling around.

He missed his mom tucking him in at night. Boiling water for macaroni and cheese on the stove and singing along with the radio, a song he'd never heard before. Telling him to stop messing with their dog Daisy and pulling her tail. "How would you like it if somebody pulled your tail?" she asked, when he wouldn't leave Daisy alone.

He missed reading aloud at night with his dad. Riding bicycles together. Throwing the football. Drawing goofy cartoons about "The Adventures of Jimbo the Clown and his Boss Ed" while they lay on the carpet with the sun on their backs, laughing at nothing. Silly stories, impossible characters. Drinking hot cocoa and eating graham crackers together. "C'mon Sam," his dad had scolded, "you're getting crumbs all over the floor."

"Sorry Dad."

"Just pick 'em up and put 'em in the sink."

Sam heard a bird singing in a nearby tree and stopped. He came back from his memory, stood in the middle of the road and scratched his head. He didn't have a clue how to find his father and nobody he ran into seemed to know either. He was hungry, thirsty too. He looked toward Belltown and saw carts and donkeys. A small cloud of dust rose from the circus in the distance. Scattered houses here and there. A couple of fellows leaning against a split rail fence up ahead. Two dogs, wandering in a ditch by the side of the road, sniffing things.

A big horse came clopping up, headed toward town. On the back of the horse was a straw-haired boy with freckles and a serious expression who reminded Sam of Terry. He held onto the reins and sat straight-backed on a faded saddle blanket. Sam watched as he went by, the horse's long tail swishing to keep flies from its flanks.

He fell in behind the horse, not too close, still watching the tail when he heard a voice, "Pssst...hey kid."

Sam looked back and saw nothing. He looked to the side of the road. There were the two fellows he'd seen leaning against the fence. They had bodies of men and the heads of crows. The shorter crow wore a frayed red plaid vest over a coarse pea-green shirt. His shoes soft, like Rubberface's. The taller one wore a black frock coat over a pale yellow shirt and dusty black boots with thick soles. Both men had mud-colored trousers. The short one had a long stem of grass in his beak.

The taller one winked at Sam and said, "Pssst, kid—over here." He scooped his hand toward his chest. "C'mere."

Sam walked over to the two men. The taller one was the younger of the two. The shorter fellow had white feathers on the sides of his head.

"My name's Marly," the taller one said. "And this here's Rufus. What's your name?"

"Sam. Sam Bixby."

"Sam," Marly repeated, "that's a good, strong name. Sturdy. You look like a strong young fellow."

"Well I—" Sam said.

"Don't go dis-agreeing with me," Marly cut in. "Might as well learn to take a compliment. They get a little scarce when you get older."

Rufus removed the stem from his mouth. "Goin' to the circus are you?" His voice was low and raspy. Marly's was higher, sharper.

"I was thinking of it," Sam answered. "How'd you guess?"

"Might be that King of Hearts in your hand," Rufus said. "Saw that fellow Osmo give it to you. He's a pretty good magician. That's *some* circus. Wouldn't miss it if I were you."

"The clowns are my favorite," Marly said. "We saw it last year. This big fat fellow riding a tiny little bicycle with a scarecrow-thin clown on his back. Thought I'd bust a gut laughing."

"I'd like to go, but, technically—" Sam managed.

"What?" Both crows said at once, peering down at Sam with great interest.

"…I'm…trying to find my dad."

Rufus squinted and nodded, a serious expression on his face. "Father's missing, eh?"

"Sorry to hear it," Marly added quietly, his voice throbbing with sympathy. "Where do you think he is?"

"That's the trouble," Sam said. "I came here from another world. Bumped my head in a cellar and somehow ended up here. I don't know how to get back."

"This *is* distressing," Rufus said, stroking his chin. "Don't see too much of that around here, do we Marly?"

"Can't say that we do, Rufus. Could be some cross-universe, seismo pollinating confabulation of the whatsis, variety. Or maybe a humpty-bumpty, frog-leg, buck and wing planetary hopscotch. Leastways that's how it looks to me."

"What?" Sam said, his head spinning.

"It could be that," Rufus replied. "Or maybe it's the sub-atomic, volcanic, reconstituted, double-fluted tonsillectomy of the cuticle cortex thrombosis revolving slowly around the umbilical hematoid whatchamacallit."

Marley nodded solemnly. "There's no question that's a possibility. Are you thinking what I'm thinking, my good man?"

"What?" Sam said, his voice rising. "What are you guys talking about?"

"Yes, I *do* believe it's possible," Rufus said, staring off toward Belltown.

"What's possible?" Sam yelled. Then he put his hand over his mouth, embarrassed. "What's possible?" he said quieter.

"The tunnel near the bridge," Marly said, "could be your only hope."

"Wish we could offer you more," Rufus added, "but that's about all—"

"Would you take me there? Do you know how to get there? Would you? Could you?" Sam was nearly breathless with excitement.

"Well, I dunno," Rufus said, looking at his wrist as if there might be a watch there. "Didn't we have some things we needed to—"

"Indeed," Marly said. "We were gonna clean the whatchahoozey, hose down the double panes and see about getting that over and under side hitch re-tooled and sand blasted so's it will finally rotate the way it ought to."

"Work, work, work," Rufus continued, shaking his head.

"Jeeze McGeeze Louise," Sam said, "I know you guys are busy, but it sure would mean the world to me if you could show me that tunnel by the bridge, or whatever it is."

The two crows looked at each other. Marly frowned.

Sam glanced over his shoulder at the road and then looked down at his dusty shoes. "Alright, I guess I can find it. I'll just ask someone else and—"

"Hold on, m'boy," Rufus said, loud enough to startle Sam. "I think we can fit you in. Whatayou say, Marly? Let's put our petty concerns aside and help someone who's truly in need for a change, eh? The boy could use a hand."

"Couldn't we all," Marly said, clapping his hand on Sam's shoulder. "We'll get you there and take care of our business tomorrow."

"It would mean an awful lot to me," Sam said.

"We're not making any promises, now," Rufus said, falling in beside them as they strolled toward Belltown. "I think that the tunnel could be your doorway to another world. Whether it's the one you came from or not...I can't say."

"Me neither," Marly said, grinning, looking at Sam.

17

Sam was so excited, his heart was about to jump out of his rib cage. He was finally getting to Belltown and the tunnel. This was a possibility, a *real* possibility. Maybe, just maybe he could get back and see his dad by suppertime. He could come back into the cabin and throw his arms around his father. Hug him and kiss him the way he liked. Surprise the heck out of him. "Did I get a hug? A kiss from my favorite boy?" his father said every time Sam came to visit. Maybe his dad wouldn't see him when he walked in. Sam could run across the kitchen and tackle him. His father wouldn't know what hit him.

Marly, Rufus and Sam passed a barn with a grey, sagging roof and huge pine trees, thick and sturdy. A few carts led by donkeys and horses rolled by, their hooves clacking on the lumpy road. The houses were closer together as they approached the town. Rufus and Marly glanced at each other a few times but didn't say a word.

"You hungry?" Marly asked Sam as they reached the edge of town.

"A little," Sam answered. "Mostly thirsty."

"How 'bout you step in our place for a minute?" Marly said. "We'll fix you up with something to drink."

"Might even give you a slice of fresh blackberry pie," Rufus chimed in.

"Yep, four and twenty blackbirds made it," Marly added.

Sam turned, a puzzled look on his face. "I thought they were *baked* in it."

Rufus quickly shook his head. "No, no, no. I know the story you're thinking of. This pie comes from the 4 and 20 Bakery on Whitmore Street, Blackbird-owned, of course."

Marly nudged Rufus and rolled his eyes. "Right. We'll just step inside for a glass of milk and a piece of pie. Then take you to the tunnel. Sound good?"

"OK," Sam replied.

They walked for another block and the two men stopped. "Well, here we are," Marly said. He waved his hand at the house as if he was introducing it to Sam. "Home sweet home."

Sam stared at the door. It had once been green but nearly all the paint had chipped off. Rufus fumbled with a key ring, picked one and opened the door.

"After you," Marly said, nodding to Sam with another sweep of his hand.

Sam glanced at the street to get his bearings. The houses were narrow, set close together and fashioned from rough wooden planks. He went in.

It was a dark single room with a window up high that faced the street and a smaller window in the back by the kitchen. The street-side window was propped up with a stick. There were two low single beds on either side of the room, a wood stove, cupboard, weathered wooden table and two rickety kitchen chairs.

"Have a seat, make yourself comfortable," Marly said. He stared at Rufus and cleared his throat. "Ahem."

"Oh…right," Rufus said. "What kind of a host am I?" He crossed the room to the kitchen and asked over his shoulder, "Piece of pie then, Sam?"

"Well, I—"

"C'mon, one piece won't hurt," Rufus said, smiling. "That bakery makes a darn fine pie."

"OK," Sam said, glancing at Rufus working in the kitchen. "Then I better be going."

"Of course," Rufus replied.

Sam looked at the slanting, fading light coming in through the window from the street. He noticed a domed metal bird cage hanging from the ceiling near it. "Do you have a bird?"

"Um… no," Marly replied quietly. "'Course we *are* part bird."

"Oh yeah," Sam said, "sorry. I didn't mean any—"

"Here's your pie, and a bit of milk to go with it," Rufus said, interrupting, setting a cup and plate in front of Sam.

Sam stared at the huge wedge of blackberry pie with a fork across the plate and the cup of milk beside it.

Marly sat down at the table and watched Sam with interest.

"Go ahead," Rufus said, standing by with his hands on his hips.

Sam took a bite. It *was* good. "Wow," he said, through a mouthful of pie.

The men nodded and grinned. "Told you," Marly said.

Sam sipped the milk. It was heavy as cream with a little foam on top. Sam ate with gusto, surprised how hungry he was. For a few minutes the only sound in the room was him chewing. Rufus went back to the kitchen, poured water into a teapot and set it on top of the stove. Marly pulled a folding knife from his pocket and began to clean the dirt beneath his fingernails.

Sam was working on the last crumbs on his plate, mashing them with the tongs of his fork, wondering if he should ask for another small piece when Marly spoke:

"You know, we *heard* about you."

Sam looked up, astonished, with the fork in his mouth tasting the last sweet crumbs. "What do you mean?"

"A little bird told us," Marly said.

"One of our smaller brothers," Rufus added. He wiped his hands on a towel, came over, and stood by the table. "Fellow by the name of Dexter. Said you gave him a licking. Threatened to do a heck of a lot more than that if he ever troubled you again."

"I don't know what you're talking about," Sam said, nervously, glancing at the door.

"He said you changed from a robin into a…a…boy," Marly said.

"This very boy before us eating pie," Rufus added.

"He was attacking me. Wouldn't share those cherries. I had to defend myself," Sam protested.

"That's not the way he told it," Rufus said.

Sam pushed his chair back. "I have to go. Thanks so much for the pie. It was delicious. I guess I was hungrier than I thought I—"

"Sit down," Marly said with a growl. He stood up from the table. "We're not gonna punish you. Dexter was a puffed-up little windbag, a real pain in the *be*-hind. He probably got what he deserved from you."

"We may be crows, but we ain't fools," Rufus put in. "He's a bully."

"We want something else from you," Marly said, leaning over Sam, his hands on the table.

"What do you mean? I don't have anything, I swear," Sam said. He didn't look at the men. The air was thick and menacing in the half-dark room. He felt like anything could happen. "I don't have any money. If I had some, you could have it all."

"We don't want your money," Marly said.

Rufus leaned in, his beak a few inches from Sam's nose. "We want your magic."

"Show us how you did it," Marly continued. "How you changed from a boy to a robin."

"*That's* what we want," Rufus said, tapping his beak. "We're partials. Body of a man, head of a crow. We want to go all the way."

"Become the men we were meant to be," Marly added.

"I don't know," Sam said, his voice quavery. "I mean, I never knew how to do this stuff before I came to this world. I'm not sure I can explain it. I guess you just have to look at something, concentrate, and...and...somehow it *happens*. It's kind of magic, really...no kidding. Now, if you'll excuse me, that's all I know. I really need to be going."

Sam pushed his chair back and stood up.

Rufus moved behind Sam and barred the door. Marly came around the table and scowled at Sam. He banged the table with the flat of his hand. "You're not going anywhere until we get what we want—your magic!" He grabbed Sam by the shoulders, pushed him down in the chair and held him there. Rufus slipped up from behind with a rope Sam hadn't noticed and wrapped it snugly around his torso.

Sam's heart jumped to his throat. He squirmed and tried to get up but Marly's big hands held him in place.

"I swear that's all I know," Sam pleaded, his voice rising in volume. His breath came in short, raspy gasps. "You gotta believe me, I—"

"Shut up, or I'll have to gag you," Marly snapped. "Wouldn't want that, would we?"

Sam held his breath. His mouth quivered like a drop of water on a hot stove. He couldn't control it. Big warm tears streamed down his cheeks. His chest shook and heaved.

"Now look what you've done," Rufus said to Marly. "Made the boy cry."

Marly squatted in front of Sam and studied his wet eyes. "We're not gonna hurt you, we want you to *help* us, that's all." He pulled a rumpled red handkerchief from his pocket and dabbed Sam's cheeks. "C'mon, show us how you do it."

Sam looked in Marly's eyes. He was trying to show sympathy, all trembly and pouting, but his eyes were glassy and bright, hard as coins.

Rufus finished tying Sam's torso so he couldn't move. "Tell me if that's too tight and uncomfortable." Then, as Marly stood up and studied his handiwork, Rufus knelt at Sam's feet and tied his legs to the chair. "Can't have you running off now, can we?"

Sam looked past Marly's head and saw a small yellow bird. It landed on the ledge of the window propped open by a stick. The men didn't seem to notice the bird. It glanced at the three figures, slipped inside, and pecked a crumb on the ledge.

Sam closed his eyes for a moment and listened to his breath. His heart tripped like a card in the spokes of a bicycle wheel. He tried to go deeper with his breath even though fear gripped his throat, chest and legs. He looked at the bird pecking crumbs. It made small, precise jumps.

Sam stayed with the bird and imagined that he was pecking too, light as a ball of cotton. That he had feathers and wings where his arms were and a tail sticking out back to balance with.

Then, before the astonished crows eyes, he became the bird on the ledge. The ropes drooped in a sagging heap on the chair.

He let out a startled chirp and the two men turned from the empty chair to the window and Sam perched there. They both understood what had happened at once and lunged for Sam.

Sam glanced at the wedge of open window and jumped. He accidentally tripped the stick holding it open with his foot. A thin strip of dust rose up and the window slammed shut, leaving him inside. Sam pecked at the glass and beat his wings furiously against it, yelling, "No, no, no," in a high, tight voice.

Then he felt a hand close around him. "Gotcha." It was Marly.

Rufus unhooked the domed metal cage from the ceiling, set it on the table and opened the small, curved door. Marly slipped his hand inside the cage and released Sam, quickly shutting the door behind him.

Sam beat his wings against the cage. He knew it was useless, but he had to flap his wings or else explode.

"Thought you'd slip out on us, did you?" Rufus said and laughed.

"Maybe now you'll teach us what you know," Marly added. He knelt in front of the cage. His eyes met Sam's. "How 'bout it?"

Sam's mind raced like a tiny engine. He glanced at Marly, then away. He was hot and his legs were so shaky he could barely stand up. His bones light, wings light and his belly light as a balloon.

He turned his back on the men and huddled in the bottom of the cage facing the window. *So close*, he thought. *I almost got away.*

He remembered his father and wondered if he'd find his way back. His dad must be sick with worry by now looking high and low. Sam wondered if he'd discovered the cellar and poked around in it. Maybe he could find a way to Sam!

He thought of Franklin, his small, dusty cabin, the masks on the wall. The sandwich he'd made, how kind he'd been. "Call me," he'd said. Sam remembered he didn't have a phone. Franklin had looked Sam in the eye, tapped his chest above his heart and said, "Call me."

I'm calling, Franklin, *I'm calling,* he thought, huddled in the cage. A yellow ball of feathers with two sad, moist eyes staring at the window and the golden fading light slanting in.

18

Sam looked at the window as if it might give him a clue about what he should do next. His chest was heavy, heart weary. His eyes blurred around the edges. Sleep pulled at him. He tried with all his might to stay awake. *I need to…I've got to…*he thought….

He slept.

When he awoke he didn't have any idea how long he'd been out. What woke him was the singing. The light was lower in the window, as if evening had crept into the room and stolen the last shafts of light. Rufus had his back to Sam, standing at the kitchen counter. He poured steaming water from a copper teapot into two cups and sang in a low, rusty voice:

> You can live by the sword
> And die by the blade
> It don't matter a'tall
> You're the ace, Ace of Spades

You'll sail pirate frigates
And rob railroad trains
Sleep out in winter
You won't mind the rain

You don't suffer boundaries
Directions or maps
Your compass is true
Dead reckoning, chaps

You don't have a family
You don't need a trade
You'll slip by, you'll get by
You're the ace, Ace of Spades

You'll never end up
Like some quivering jelly
Crawlin' through life
In the dirt on your belly

You live by the sword
You die by the blade
Who cares what they think?
You're the ace, Ace of Spades

Marly came up behind Rufus and whispered, "Shhhh...you'll wake the boy, the bird, whatever."

"Right," Rufus whispered back. "So, what'll we do? Can't keep him locked up forever."

Huddling in his cage, Sam listened to every word they said. The men didn't seem to notice.

"I don't know," Marly said. "We've got to make a plan. I figure he'll see the error of his ways, 'fore long. He helps us, we set him free—

right?"

Rufus nodded and handed a cup to Marly. "Might have to wear him down a bit."

Marly took the tea. "You leave that to me. In the meantime I say… Ruf, old boy, the circus is in town. I don't know about you, but I could sure go for some gut-busting clown action. Maybe a high-wire act or two. Whattayou say?"

"Suits me. What about our friend?" Rufus cocked his head toward the cage.

"Bring 'em. He's not going anywhere."

"Right." Rufus turned, glanced at the cage and saw Sam blink. "Well, look who's up—Mr. Sunshine."

The men came over to Sam with the cups steaming in their hands.

"Ready to show us?" Marly asked, smiling.

Sam looked back without blinking.

"I see," Marly said. He reached behind Sam, pulled something off the shelf, went to the table and sat down. It was a deck of cards. He shuffled them. They fluttered against the table as he hummed the Ace of Spades song.

Then he turned the deck over and went through the cards one by one as if he was looking for something. "Here it is, the King of Hearts. My good man," he said to Rufus, "I believe we have a ticket."

Rufus had been watching Sam. He turned and laughed when he saw the card.

Marly slipped the card in his coat pocket, crossed the room and unhooked Sam's cage from a nail on the ceiling. He peered in and grinned. "My fine-feathered friend, we're going to take a little trip."

Sam stopped himself from answering.

Marly nodded to Rufus and muttered, "Boy's not curious. What is it with kids these days?" He peered in at Sam. "You should be excited m'boy. You're going to the circus."

The men crossed the room to the door. Sam glanced down at the table. He noticed the Ace of Spades had slipped from the deck when Marly shuffled the cards. It was wedged between the seat and back of the chair like a tiny stiff flag.

19

The street was bustling with activity. Sam jumped up on the perch and held on tight so he wouldn't be thrown and miss what was going on.

There were wagons, horses, people walking this way and that. The sounds of footsteps, voices, hoof beats, the cooing of doves and the creak of the cage as it swung by Marly's side. No one seemed to think it odd the men were carrying a cage down the street with a bird in it.

"D'you think he'll try to escape?" Rufus asked.

Marly shook his head. "He knows better."

"Why's that?"

"Two reasons. First, if he goes back to being Sam right now, he'll be stuffed in that cage like a plump turkey. And second, if he turns himself into something else, he may not be able to get back to being Sam. You remember the story of old Ed Stubbins don't you?"

"Can't say I do."

"Well, his wife chased him out the house and down the street one night on accounta he'd been drinking with his buddies. Don't know why this particular night, she'd seen it all before. Anyway, she chased him over a stone bridge."

"Yeah?"

"He figures he'll jump and he does. Problem is, the old sot can't swim. Then he gets a brilliant idea, he'll turn himself into a fish, swim his way out of trouble."

"And?"

"He does. Then his wife comes down, sees he's a fish and reaches in to grab him. He changes to a crawdad at the last minute, crawls under a rock. She can't find him. When she's gone, he creeps out. Tries to turn back into Ed—no dice. He *did* turn back into a fish. Better a fish than a crawdad I guess."

"Well I'll be."

"Saw him years later," Marly said. "I was bending over the river to take a drink and there he was. Still had a bit of old Stubbin's face to him, you know, big nose and all. He swims right up to me, pokes that snout out of the water and says, 'Marly, it's *me*, Ed. You remember me don'tcha? You gotta help me.' 'How am I gonna do that,' I says. 'Lookit me Ed, I'm halfway there myself.' "

"He blubbered like a baby," Marly continued. "Pitiful thing to see a fish cry. Don't know where the tears stop and the river begins. Anyway, I shrugged. What could I do?"

"If you drink like a fish, you end *up* one, I guess," Rufus said, laughing at his own joke.

Marly laughed too and winked at Rufus. The men walked up to the entrance to the circus. It was an enormous, dull-yellow canvas tent. Marly presented the King of Hearts to a fellow with the body of a man and the face of a sad-looking beagle in a black frock coat.

The beagle said, "Osmo's guests are you? Go on in, sit anywhere you like."

The men wove through the crowd and found an empty section of wooden benches ten rows from the stage. They sat down with the cage between them. The tent was thick with voices, the stage was a large dirt circle flecked with straw. In the circle were red, yellow and blue risers that looked like large squat cans. There were swings overhead for the acrobats and ropes leading up to huge poles that supported the peaks of the tent.

To the right of the stage Sam could make out some of the musicians he'd seen earlier. The Donkey man, Fox fellow, Panda and Gorilla were all there. The bearded man in woman's dress blew a few long low blats on the trombone and fussed with the slide.

Sam was depressed. His heart thumped, a low, sad drumbeat. He thought of becoming a bat, an insect, anything that could help him escape once they got to the circus. He figured he'd make his break from the men when the clowns were on stage and they were distracted. He hadn't counted on Marly's story about Ed Stubbins who ended up living as a fish in the river with no way out.

He realized he could get trapped too if he wasn't careful, maybe even if he was. He might end up a spider, house cat, dog or dragonfly with no way to get back to Sam and no way to return to his father.

Then again, what if he stayed a bird? Was there a time limit? Stay a bird too long and you can't come back? Either way was dangerous. If he expanded back into Sam right now, he'd be stuffed inside the cage, maybe break a leg, or worse. He slumped in the cage, dejected.

The orchestra began to play, twisting melodies wrapped around one another like wild tree vines, climbing higher and higher. The Gorilla, pounded out a thumping, lumpy drumbeat. The otter crashed the cymbals willy-nilly. The Fox man blew shimmering bright sprays of trumpet notes like gold coins falling from the sky.

A man with a megaphone strode to the center of the dirt floor stage with a whip in his hand. He wore a dusty top hat and black tuxedo. His handlebar moustache was waxed and curved to the ceiling. He brought the cone to his lips, raised the whip over his head and brought it down with a snap.

The orchestra miraculously fell silent, right on the beat. Everyone except the otter, who clapped two great cymbal crashes after everyone had stopped.

The man in the top hat glared at the otter, who shrugged and hung his head in shame. The audience erupted in hoots, hollers and laughter. Some of them even made paper airplanes out of the programs and sailed them to the stage. One landed at the ringmasters feet. His face glowed red beneath the lights as if he was about to pop.

He managed a tight smile, cleared his throat and said, "Ah...an enthusiastic audience. Just the kind we like. My name is Oscar Von Huffenbach, master of ceremonies. What you are about to see is the greatest collection of circus talent ever to grace the face of this planet—the world's finest. We've brought together jugglers from Effluvia, master musicians from Cornucopia, clowns from Bellagio, Spotsylvania and Pistol River. You'll see sights you've never seen before. Things you only imagined in story books. Feats of daring-do, impossibly difficult acts of juggling, and death-defying deeds featuring the Lioness Von Baroness of Pyromania performing her high-wire tight rope ballet."

"Ah, shaddup and bring on the clowns," shouted a short, stout man with a bald head and chin whiskers who sat near the front.

The crowd roared. Oscar shook his head, scowled at the man and raised his whip above his head. Silence. Then Oscar snapped the whip and the show began.

A bear on a bicycle pedaled out to center stage and made loops around the circle. The band played low in the background, a woozy waltz number that rose and fell with his feet on the pedals.

A dancing bear couple waltzed out and gracefully swirled to the center of the stage. The bear on the bicycle took hold of the pedals with his forepaws and began pushing them up and down, slowly lifting his hindquarters until he was standing upside down working them in time with the dancers, his back feet in the air. The waltzing bears separated and the bear on the bicycle rode through them. Then they came back together.

The band sped up until the couple was twirling at center stage and the bicycle bear rode around them like a one-creature merry-go-round, his legs a blur. They all stopped at once, the bears and the orchestra. The tent was quiet for a moment and then erupted in cheers and shouting.

The clowns were next. A baggy pants man with frizzy orange hair and a woman with a snake on her head. The man had a water bottle and ran in circles squirting the kids in the front row with it. He hit a stout grizzled fellow in red suspenders and the man jumped up, enraged, and tore after the clown. The clown ran faster. Before long the man was huffing and puffing behind him. The man stopped to catch his breath. The clown woman tapped him on the shoulder and smiled. Then the frizzy-haired clown gave the man a shot in the face with his water bottle. The man blew his stack and howled, "I'll get you...you...you consarned, darn-blarn-back-wallow-flib-willow-frizzy-haired-good-for-nothing clown." He stomped his feet in the dirt. His suspenders sprang up and snapped him in the face.

The crowd went nuts, hooting, hollering, shouting, throwing

popcorn and peanut shells.

The man wiped water off his face with his shirt sleeve and chased the frizzy-haired clown again, more furious than before.

The woman clown stood in the center of the stage with her hands on her hips. The orchestra began a throbbing pulse like a soundtrack for a long desert caravan. With the music grooving, the snake rose up from the woman's head and swayed in time with it.

While the angry man chased the frizzy-haired clown around the stage another clown in pink came in from the back. He was short, round, and rode a pig. The pig pulled a fat cannon on wheels behind it. The pink clown whacked the pig's flanks to keep it moving. The pig glared at the clown on its back, grunted and stopped near the lady with the snake on her head. The snake bobbed in time with the music and the woman's hips did too.

The pink clown shrugged, got off the pig and unhooked the cannon. He walked over to the angry man and held up his hand for the man to stop. The angry man stopped to catch his breath and the pink clown slipped his hand in his loose, full coat and produced a daisy. He presented it to the angry man, whose frown disappeared with the gesture. He shook his head and turned to leave when the pink clown tapped him on the shoulder. He swung around and was surprised to find he was facing the cannon. The woman clown had lit the fuse. The crowd held their breath as the man's expression turned from shock to fear to fury. It seemed to Sam that any moment steam might come from the man's ears.

Then the cannon exploded with a crack and a great cloud of green smoke poofed from the barrel. When it cleared, the angry man rubbed his eyes with one hand, the other still clutching the daisy.

A pint-sized clown with a small pointed hat poked his head out of the cannon. He had a squirt bottle in his hand and spritzed the angry man in the face.

The man lunged at the clown in the cannon but missed. He staggered, tripped, and fell face first in the dust, sending up a small cloud.

Then he stood, enraged. His front was caked in mud and straw, his suspenders dangled at his sides. "I'll get you...you...you CLOWNS!" he shouted, as they hurried off stage.

The man stumbled after them to the open flap in the back of the tent where the performers came through. Then he backed up before a beefy, well-built fellow wearing a leopard skin loin cloth and iron bracelets around his wrists. His head was shaved and he had a waxed black mustache and earring.

A strongman, Sam guessed. He kept coming at the angry man who backed up. The strong man frowned and pointed to the benches. The angry man reluctantly returned to his seat.

Then the orchestra struck up a stately march and a big man came through the tent flap entrance. He had the head of a bison with short, curved horns, great black eyes and a wavy beard on his chin. His shoulders were broad as a doorway. He wore tall boots and loose pants. A vest covered his thick, hairy torso. Perched on one shoulder was a small, beautifully-formed woman in a white dress. She had doll-like features, a tiny mouth with pale pink lips and plump arms and legs. She held a small house in her hands tenderly, as if it contained something special.

The bison man stepped to the center of the circle and stopped. The orchestra stopped with him. Then, softly, they began a waltz. A delicate thing, sweet as meringue. The bison held his left hand flat and the doll woman placed the house on his palm gently. Then he brought the house around in front of him. His hand was bigger than the house. He placed his right hand next to his left, also palm up.

The door to the house opened and a tiny ballerina emerged. She couldn't have been more than five inches high, Sam guessed. She wore pink tights, ballet slippers and a pink ruffled skirt. She leapt to the bison's right hand and began to twirl on his outstretched palm. She jumped out to each finger and back to his palm in time to the music.

The crowd was unusually quiet. They leaned in to see better. People in the back stood up on their benches.

The ballerina began to spin. Slowly at first and then faster and faster. At first, with one knee out and both hands over her head. Then she lowered an arm and raised her leg until it was over her head, still spinning.

The orchestra followed her and sped up the waltz until it was a wheezing, breathing rush.

Sam watched the dancer closely as she became a blur on the man's hand. The music seemed to lift higher and higher until it was pushing at the top of the tent as if it might break through. The doll woman stood on the bison's shoulder, opened her mouth and began to sing. Her beautiful soprano lifted with the music until it, too, rose to the top of the tent. When they reached the highest note, her voice and the orchestra hovered for a moment, then stopped. So did the ballerina, as if she was frozen, a snapshot in time, her leg still up in the air. Then she let go and gracefully brought it down to rest on the bison's hand.

The crowd exploded. Whistling, stomping their feet and howling their approval.

The ballerina bowed, turned and went back inside the house. The bison lifted it to the doll woman. She cradled it in her arms and sat down on his shoulder. Then, he nodded, turned and vanished through the flap from which he'd come.

As soon as he was gone, five dogs came out, all walking upright on their hind legs. They rolled large, red, yellow and blue balls made of light wood or metal, Sam guessed. The dogs were followed by five jugglers, shirtless, dressed in loose, olive drab pants and red velvet vests trimmed in yellow. They had the bodies of men and the heads of monkeys. One monkeyman juggled knives, another pins, another bright red balls, the fourth kept three lit torches spinning in front of him. And last, the tallest man juggled birds. Round, pale yellow birds that didn't seem to mind being tossed in the air.

The dogs rolled their balls out to the stage and made a circle. They mounted the shifting balls and stood atop them. One dog nearly slid off. Then they began to roll the balls with their feet, keeping their heads erect, looking straight ahead. When the dogs had established a rhythm, the jugglers formed a circle outside the one the dogs made. One by one they went from the outer circle to the inner and then back again, weaving a pattern.

Sam was stunned. It was as if the circles were breathing, expanding, contracting. They looked like a slowed-down top spinning, each part ebbing and flowing.

Then, each of the performers left the circle: dog, monkey, dog, monkey, until they formed a line leaving the stage. The dogs were still atop the balls rolling them skillfully with their feet.

The orchestra signaled a change with a brassy fanfare, then settled into a long, thick chord while a drummer began a roll with his sticks rattling on the snare. He picked up speed, faster, faster, faster. The orchestra brought the volume up with him, swelling. The musicians seemed to be climbing over one another to get to the top of a great heap. Then climax—crescendo—silence.

All eyes were on the opening in back where the performers entered.

It was the Lioness von Baroness of Pyromania. She walked to the center of the stage, her head high. She wore a pale green velvet robe with gold trim. Four monkeys in vests walked behind her supporting her train.

Then, they pulled her robe back, came together in a dance-like move, folded the robe and walked off the stage with it tucked beneath their arms.

The lioness stood motionless for a moment. Her pointed ears twitched, chin up, gaze fierce. She had the body of a well-developed woman with big breasts and broad hips. Her arms and thighs were strong and firm. She wore a low-cut top of pale blue with gold trim. On her hips was a short skirt with sharp gold folds that reflected the light, slicing it up like a knife.

She held out her arms, palms up, bowed slightly and walked to a ladder hanging from a tall pole on the side of the stage. She climbed until she reached a small round platform near the top.

The drummer began a whispering roll and the orchestra swelled to a dense chord that went on and on, gradually building to a thick ball of tension.

The lioness wore soft leather slippers. She stepped off the platform onto the high wire. It trembled under her weight. She placed one foot after another until she was half-way across the wire, balancing with her arms outstretched. It seemed to Sam that she was holding up the entire audience with her broad arms. All of them supported by her feet on the wire, quivering in the air.

The crowd was quiet as a cemetery. No one whispered. Sam was having trouble breathing and lowered his eyes. He saw the back of someone sitting on a bench three rows ahead and felt a familiar jolt. Those shoulders, that wild crop of bristly hair. That mud-colored coat. It was eerie. It was…it was….

The man turned his head, peeked at Sam and winked—Franklin!

Sam wanted to flap his wings and shout to him but the sound stuck in his throat. He made a choked cluck instead. Rufus and Marly glared at him and frowned. "Shhh," Rufus said, holding his fingers to his beak.

Sam glanced down, but not before shooting Franklin a look. Franklin snapped his head back to the front and then gazed up at the lioness as if nothing happened.

Sam peeked at Marly and Rufus. Their attention was back on the lioness. They didn't seem to notice Franklin.

The lioness continued her high wire act. The audience oohed and ahhhed, but Sam could think of nothing but the old man three rows in front of him. He'd come!

There were a few routines after hers. One featured elephants in a pyramid with the one on top twirling a ball at the end of his trunk. Then more clowns, jugglers and the strongman came out for the finale, bent an iron bar with his teeth and held up a man and woman from the audience while the crowd cheered and stood on their seats. They threw popcorn and peanuts at the stage and gave a standing ovation.

Rufus lifted the cage and they stood up to leave. Sam jumped on his perch and jerked his head back and forth, frantically searching the faces and backs of people to catch a glimpse of Franklin.

Franklin caught Sam's eye, mouthed the words, "I'll follow you," and looked away before Rufus or Marly noticed.

With the cage between them, the two crows fell in with the crowd as they spilled out of the tent onto the street. "Great show," Rufus said.

Sam faced the back of the cage and scanned the crowd, looking for Franklin.

"Greatest on earth," Marly replied, studying Sam. "He's been awfully quiet. Not a peep out of the bird."

"Facing the wrong way, too. What's eating you boy?" Rufus asked, giving the cage a jerk and bringing it up to his eyes.

Sam stared back at him. "I've got nothing to say to you two."

Marly laughed. "I think we've upset the dear boy."

"No doubt," Rufus replied. "He'll come 'round. Give him time."

20

They wound their way through the crowd and returned to the house. Marly opened the door. It was dark and stuffy inside. He lit a candle and Rufus hung the cage from a hook near the front window. Then he propped it open with a stick.

"Wouldn't do that," Marly said. "Our friend might decide to do something foolish and fly the coop."

"Right." Rufus removed the prop. "Smells like the inside of an old shoe in here, though."

"Probably your careless housekeeping," Marly said. "Time for a drink." He reached over the stove and pulled a jug and two clay cups down from a shelf. "To celebrate."

"Celebrate what?" Rufus said.

"Why...our freedom. I've got a feeling our friend Sam will see the error of his ways, come 'round to what's best for him, best for us and 'fore you know it...we'll be men. No more of this half and half business."

Marly poured two cups of whisky and offered one to Rufus.

"I'll drink to that," Rufus said, clicking Marly's cup with his own. "Smoke?"

"Sure, a little whisky and tobacco suits me fine."

They drank and chatted, both puffing away at corncob pipes.

Sam coughed, and looked out the window. His eyes stung with smoke. He shut them tight and thought of Franklin, wondering what he'd do. *If* he'd show up. What he'd look like. Sam's chest was tight from the foul air. He was exhausted from stress and confinement in the cage. He wondered if he had the chance to escape if he'd be able to turn himself back into a boy again and get free of these rascals. He stared through the bars at the window, his throat dry as a dusty cornstalk. Hope flickered in his chest. He didn't want to miss Franklin. Then, a gentle wave slipped over him and swept him away...he slept.

He dreamt that he was on a huge ferryboat with his father. The sun was shining and they were going back home to Vashon Island. The sky was turquoise. Millions of tiny waves rippled like silverbacked fish as he looked over the side of the great vessel steaming toward the island they lived on—home.

He awoke with a start. He had fallen asleep on the perch and nearly fell off it head first onto the floor of the cage. When his eyes blinked open he almost yelled. A spider hung a few inches in front of his face from the top of the cage.

One of the spider's legs went to its mouth. "Shhhh," it whispered, "it's *me*, Franklin."

Sam stared at the small dark shape and miniature whiskered face before him. It was Franklin, no doubt about it. Franklin grinned and cocked his head, "Look behind you, Sammy."

Sam heard muffled snoring and turned. The candle was a stub on the table, wax ringed its thin, wavering flame, the jug beside it without a stopper. The men had fallen asleep at the table, Sam guessed. Marly's head turned to the side, one eye open and glassy. Rufus faced away, his arms embraced the table as if it was his pillow. With the exception of their heads, both men were covered with thousands of silvery webs.

Their legs were wrapped with countless strands wound 'round the chair legs.

"Quiet now," Franklin cautioned. "We'll talk later. First thing's first. I gotta work on this lock."

He lowered himself to the base of the cage, slid between the thin metal bars and crawled over the dull brass lock on the door.

He slipped in the key slot and disappeared. Sam heard faint ticks and clicks as he worked in the dark. There was a snap. Sam held his breath, realizing that Franklin could be killed if a spring unwound and crushed him against the inside chamber of the lock.

Then there was a loud click and the hoop snapped open. Franklin staggered out of the slot and shook his head, dazed. He'd survived!

Marly snorted and Rufus belched and stirred. He tried to stretch his arms, jerked his head and exclaimed, "What the? Marly wake up, wake up! We're all tied up."

Marly lifted his head from the top of the table. His arms didn't budge, they were wrapped in spiderwebs, his legs bound to the chair. He clawed at the webs, kicked his legs and made his chair buck like a boxy wooden horse making short, clumsy jumps. Then, he teetered on two legs and went over backward. "Whoa…no…ouch!" he yelped, crashing to the floor.

Rufus freed his hands and tore at the webs binding his legs. He glanced up at Sam and saw him perched at the open door of the cage. "He's free, Marly—FREE!"

"Well…get him," Marly snarled, kicking his legs on the floor in a fit.

"You get him," Rufus snapped, "I'm tryin' to get outta this mess same as you."

Sam jumped to the window and Franklin swung up to the ledge on a fine thread behind him. "Push the window open, Sam—now."

"Y'hear that?" Rufus said. "He's got somebody with him, the little creep."

"Probably the spider that tied us up," Marly said, thrashing and thumping on the floor. "Rufus…I got my legs out now, workin' on my hands."

"Keep goin', they're gonna fly the coop on us," Rufus replied, huffing and puffing.

Sam pushed the pane of glass with his small, feathered shoulder and felt it budge. It was heavy but creaked open. He saw the street below, cobblestones gleaming in the moonlight.

"Keep pushing, Sammy. Don't stop," Franklin urged behind him.

"You're stronger than me right now."

"Doing the best I can." Sam gave a mighty push and the window sprang free. He held it open with his back to it. "Hurry, Franklin. I can't keep doing this, it's heavier than I am."

"I'm coming," Franklin answered, scurrying along the ledge. He was almost free from the window when Sam said, "Uh-oh." He lost control of the window. It swung back toward Franklin. Franklin scampered fast as his eight legs would carry him, but the wood frame swooshed by, clipped him on the shoulder and landed on one of his legs pinning him at the base of the window.

"Ouch...that smarts. Quick Sammy, get this thing off me."

Sam hopped to the ledge, grabbed the small round fastening hook with his feet, flapped his wings and pulled with all his might. He heard the men cursing, crashing and thrashing about inside trying to get free.

His yellow wings were a fluttering blur struggling against the dusty window. It lifted.

"Atta boy, atta boy," Franklin yelled, dragging himself clear. "You did it."

Sam looked as Franklin rubbed his leg.

"Hope it's not broke," Franklin said.

"Me too. Hop on my back. I'll get us down to the street."

"Good idea," Franklin said, climbing delicately on Sam's back. "OK, m'boy...let's fly!"

"Hang on tight," Sam said. He spread his wings and sailed off the ledge. He wasn't sure exactly which way to go. Probably where there weren't so many people who might get suspicious of a yellow bird and a spider flying together. Sam sailed low over the rooftops passing chimneys with smoke curling out of them, peaked and thatched roofs and the tops of trees, their dark leaves shimmering in the moonlight.

"There's a good spot," Franklin said. "Little patch of green with a tree on it."

"OK," Sam said, coming in for a landing in the damp grass.

"Let's change back, my friend," Franklin said, "'fore we get in any more trouble. I'm feelin' itchy and hungry and I'd rather not go lookin' for flies right now." He clambered off Sam's back and stood on a broad, weedy leaf. "Here goes."

Franklin brought his thoughts back to his human journey. He began to fill like a balloon and lose his dark, bristly limbs. In a few moments he was standing in the grass, staring down at his leg with a frown on his face.

Sam was working too. Breathing, remembering his father, their fishing trip. Then Franklin's cabin, with its assortment of masks on the wall. "Jeezy-peezy," he exclaimed, swelling, coming back to his body. "Didn't know if I'd *ever* get back. I was worried I'd spend the rest of my life in that smelly cage."

"That's why I came," Franklin said, smiling. "Couldn't have that."

"I can't believe you're here," Sam said. He was nearly trembling with excitement in the cool night air. He rushed over to Franklin and hugged the stocky man.

Franklin returned the hug, then stepped back. "Careful son." He lifted his pant leg and looked down at his ankle. "Ahhh, that's a nasty bruise. Can't see much in this low light, but it *feels* purple and it's throbbing like a beating heart."

"Can you walk?"

Franklin hobbled a few steps. His leg sprang back up every time it touched the ground as if he'd stepped on something hot. "I'm not gonna win any races, I can tell you *that*."

Sam was silent.

Franklin looked at him and waited until their eyes met. "You go on, son. I'll tell you how to get to the tunnel under the bridge. It's not far but you better hurry. Those goons will be after you 'fore you know it. I must admit, that was one sweet job tying those boys up. I had help. Some spiders that were only too happy to join in the fun. Apparently they'd lost a lot of their brothers and sisters 'cause Rufus ran around the place and squashed 'em with a broom." He shook his head at the memory.

Sam's face was serious. "But I...I can't just leave you here. What if they come after me? What if they find you? What'll they do to you?"

"Well, they only know me as a spider but they might recognize my voice. If they do, they'll probably kill me or hurt me so's I don't feel like livin'."

"But you're already hurt. You have to come with me," Sam pleaded, his voice cracked and raw.

Franklin looked at the ground. "You better go. I'll just slow you down."

Sam stood in front of Franklin and put his hands on the older man's shoulders. "You saved my life. I'm not just gonna leave you here, OK?"

Franklin studied the boy's wild eyes. They were moist and shiny. He saw a small moon floating in each one, as if they were miniature pools. "Alright, I'll come. We're in this adventure together." He gripped Sam's shoulder with one hand and shook Sam's hand with the other. "Let's go, pardner. I'll get us there, I promise. But I won't be too darn fast about it."

21

Franklin led the way, limping down the dark streets with the boy by his side. As they walked, the old man's stride lengthened and his leg seemed to get better, Sam noticed, surprised. They passed shuttered windows with lights blinking through slats. Sam saw a circus poster already curling at the edges tacked to a fat pole.

Loud voices and laughter came from an open tavern door. There was a crash inside. A wooden chair came sailing into the street followed by a creature with the body of a man and the head of a goose. He landed with a thump face down in the dirt in front of Sam and Franklin. He moaned and didn't move, probably drunk.

"And don't come back again, y'hear?" A stout fellow bellowed from the doorway. He had a dirty apron around his waist, bare arms the size of hams and the face of a bulldog. He clapped his hands softly together as if he was washing them, turned, and headed back in the bar. "Silly goose," he muttered.

"Ouch," the goose said, lifting his head, gently touching the tip of his beak. "That smarts. I think I might've broke it."

"Let us help you up," Franklin said. He knelt down and took the man's arm. Sam grabbed the other and they lifted. The man was shaped like a light bulb with the round end on the bottom. Medium-sized, but surprisingly light.

"Thank you gentlemen," the goose said, his arms flapped as he brushed off the front of his dusty pin-striped suit. "Much obliged. Harvey Blount at your service. Former member of the Royal Fowling Mounted Fusiliers." He bowed, nearly tipped over and stood up quickly, wobbling. "Now I...I sell things for a living."

"Sell things?" Sam asked.

"Household goods, pots, pans, knives, soap, needles, thread, candles. Notions, potions, cures for what ails you. Headaches? Heartbreaks? Got the shakes? I have what your looking for. Whatever your heart desires. Our motto? *Sometimes it's the little things that make life worth living.* I'll tell you friends, I've been thither and yon, just about every dot upon the ever-loving map. Why, if it's a town, I've been there, and sometimes…" he added with a wink and a smirk, slapping his back pocket, "done that."

"I'm Franklin and this is Sam," Franklin said, "and we're in a bit of a hurry, Harvey. We're on our way to the tunnel near the bridge."

"That so?" Harvey said. His eyes drooped and he nodded, weaving slightly.

"I'm trying to remember," Franklin continued, "I believe if we keep going straight on this street and head left on Locust that will take us there. Is that right?"

"Rrrrright you are, sir," Harvey replied. His hands fluttered at his neck as if he was adjusting a necktie. "The tunnel used to be for a train but it doesn't come through here anymore. Not much of anything comes through here anymore." He stared up the dark street lost in thought for a moment and shook his head. "Best be careful. Some scruffy characters live 'round there."

"We'll look out," Franklin answered. "Thanks for the warning."

"Glad I could help," Harvey said. "Sure you fellas couldn't use a bar of soap, a fine thimble, a special bottle of lose-your-inhibitions-but-not-your-friends magical elixir? Or, how 'bout a magnificent set of the sharpest knives you'll find anywhere? Great for steaks, cakes and clambakes. Why, you'll never have to—"

"No thanks." Franklin nodded to Sam. "Let's go."

Sam paused, "I…uh, have a question."

"What?" Harvey asked. His eyes were glassy and moist and his face swam above Sam's.

"They call this place Belltown. I don't get it. I don't hear any bells."

Harvey looked off in the distance at a dark, gloomy tower. "Used to be bells, lots of 'em. A big one would ring in that yonder tower, then another, then another. 'Fore you knew it, the whole darn town was ringing. You could hear 'em for miles…reallllly something. The big one gave out a few years back. Don't know what happened to the rest of 'em. Maybe people lost interest, just didn't care. 'Course, you could

say that about a lotta things. You either care or you don't. Wanta throw
your arms around this life or shake your head and walk away. I mean,
look at me— "

Franklin jerked his head toward the tunnel, anxious to be going.

"OK," Sam said, looking at the tower, then Franklin, "thanks."

"Take care," Harvey said, waving as they walked away.

"We will," Sam said.

"Salesmen," Franklin said, shaking his head, limping briskly along.
"Sell the apron off their mother in the kitchen while she's cooking." He
looked up at a weathered wooden sign with Locust on it and pointed.
"That's it. Don't know about this tunnel, Sam. He's probably right
about keeping our eyes open though. Always pays to do that."

The buildings were closer together and more shack-like on Locust
street. Sam guessed it was a poor part of town. The road dipped down
gradually and the river came into view behind a tall wooden building with some of its windows knocked out. Bats swooshed from the
window like a vibrating black cloud. The river flowed by, the moon
swimming and flickering on its rippling surface. There was a bridge
across it made of great cubes of stone set one on top of another. Sam
wondered how they'd done it. A man in a cart pulled by a donkey
rolled slowly over the bridge away from them.

"There's the old railroad tracks," Franklin said, "and this looks like
our final destination." He pointed to the tunnel. They walked up the
road toward it. It was about twelve feet tall, Sam guessed.

"Looks more like a cave than a tunnel," Sam said, feeling a little
queasy.

"It's certainly dark as one," Franklin replied. "Well, we might as
well go spelunking."

"Spelunking?"

"That's when you enter a cave and kind of feel your way along. You
know...exploring."

"Oh."

Franklin laughed. "Which is pretty much what we're doing. We'll need a light my young friend." He pulled his hat and a candle from the folds of his coat. He produced a match, lit the candle, let wax drip on his crumpled hat and twisted the candle down in it until it stuck. "There. I'll be able to keep my hands free if need be."

He pulled another candle from his pocket, lit it and handed it to Sam. "One for you and one for me. Don't let that drip on your hand, might burn."

"I'll be careful," Sam replied, remembering the time he'd touched a pool of hot wax on a candle his father lit. It was Christmas. His father had a fire going in their wood stove and Sam was messing with the candle, dipping his fingers in a small pool near the flame. His father asked him to stop. He was dripping wax on the carpet. When Sam drew his fingers back, his dad grabbed him by the shoulder in a half hug, and tousled his hair. It seemed like nothing at the time but now Sam felt a pang. A few tears leaked from his eyes and slid down his cheeks leaving a cool snaky trail. He felt a strong urge to get going, wherever they were headed.

"Let's go then," Franklin said, turning to the dark opening.

"I'm right behind," Sam said, taking a deep breath.

22

When they entered the tunnel Sam felt a chill. The walls were rough-cut stones fit together like a giant's cubed puzzle. They glistened in the low light. Sam touched a wall and felt dampness on his fingertips.

At their feet were the bones of the old railroad track. Silvery rails with rusty patches sitting on top of cracked wooden ties sunk in gravel.

Franklin peered into the darkness ahead. "Not sure exactly what we're looking for, Sam. Hope we'll have the good sense to know it when we see it."

"What are those lights up ahead?" Sam asked, pointing to faint glowing balls wavering in the sides of the tunnel.

"Don't know," Franklin replied.

They came closer and could see they were small lamps set back in the stone walls.

"Nice of them to light our way. 'Course I don't know who *them* might be," Franklin whispered.

"You think somebody lives here?"

"Haven't a clue. Someone or something likes a little light in this place, that's for sure. Probably so they don't bump into things in the dark."

Sam noticed there were paths leading off the main train track into the sides of the tunnel. "Where do you think those things go?"

Franklin shook his head. "This is my one and only time here, Sam. Sure are black, aren't they?"

"No kidding."

The tunnel curved gradually to the left. Franklin stopped on the tracks for a moment. "Hear that?"

"What?"

"Footsteps behind us. Sounds like two people. Hope it's not who I think it is."

"You mean?"

"Our crow-headed friends. Look, over there." Franklin pointed to a rough-looking cave in the side of the tunnel. "Let's duck in here for a moment. I got a feeling. Better safe than...you know...." Franklin put his fingers to his lips. "Shhh. Follow me and douse your candle."

Franklin took off his hat and pressed the lit flame between his fingers. Sam spit on his fingertips and did the same as the footsteps came closer.

They slipped into the cave. Franklin's head cleared the cave by a foot or so.

"You sure they came here?" said a voice. "Could've gone anywhere, you know."

"He thinks this is the way back to his old man," the other voice said and laughed. "Sheesh...kids, you gotta love 'em. Believe anything you say."

It was them—Marly and Rufus! Sam's heart sank to his feet and then came bouncing back up to his chest where it beat so hard and fast he thought it might explode.

Franklin held his fingers to his lips as the two men passed.

"It's too blame dark in here, Marly. Barely see the beak in front of my face."

"Think they took one of these side caves?"

"Could be. There's plenty of 'em. We might be here all night on this godforsaken goose chase."

Sam watched them pass. Rufus held a lantern in his hand and Marly a stout-looking walking stick which clacked on the ties in an off-beat rhythm with his footsteps.

Their shadows wobbled as they passed down the tunnel following its curve.

"That was close," Franklin whispered, when they were out of earshot. He pulled off his hat, snapped a match with his thumb and lit the candle stub.

"I'll say," said a voice behind them.

Franklin and Sam started and jerked around like puppets to see what was behind them. "What the?" Franklin said, his voice low and raspy.

"Hello," the fellow said. He was almost Sam's height with the head of a frog and the body of a boy. His clothes were dark and ragged, in need of a wash. His face was smooth and green with pale yellow

circles around his broad mouth and big shiny eyes. He blinked at the candle. "Sorry," he said, his hands folded together in front of him as if he was waiting for something. "Didn't mean to scare you. My name's Frogboy."

Franklin rubbed his forehead and eyes with his fingertips and sighed deeply. "Scared the stuffing out of us, Frogboy. My name is Franklin and this here's Sam."

"Nice shoes," Frogboy said to Sam.

They shook hands all around. Franklin told Frogboy about Sam's journey, his desire to get back to his father and how they escaped the crows by transforming themselves.

"Can you help me?" Sam asked Frogboy when Franklin was finished.

Frogboy considered Sam for a moment. "Don't know. I'll try. People say there's magic in these tunnels and I don't doubt it. I've seen some of it. One of the tunnels goes to the fire room. Another to the magic pool. One of the caves opens right out over the river. Pretty place to go when the nights are clear like this and the moon is full."

"A magic pool?" Franklin asked. "Can you take us there?"

Frogboy nodded. Then he looked down the tunnel where the two crows passed. "I *know* those guys, seen 'em around town working the angles. They're no good, couple'a land pirates. They're partials just like me. Not everyone wants to be human like you two." He paused. "I must admit I do. Made it part way there, worked hard in school and had a kind teacher by the name of Mr. Gibbons who helped me. I nearly got there but he…he *died*. Never completed my training. Got everything but the head." He tapped his forehead. "Fellas think you can help me?"

"Maybe," Franklin answered. "Help us find that magic pool and we'll see what we can do."

"I'll help if I can," Sam said. "I want to find that pool too. I miss my father."

"I know what that's like," Frogboy said. "I lost me Ma and Pa when

I was just a tadpole. Large mouth bass ate 'em."

"Sorry," Sam said, shaking his head.

"Not as sorry as *I* am," Frogboy said.

"We better get going," Franklin said. "You lead the way, Frogboy."

23

They left the side tunnel. Franklin held the candle out before them as they crept along the railroad tracks.

Sam looked at the back of Frogboy's head bobbing in the low light. He heard odd sounds in the tunnel. Scraping, rustling, drips and taps. Even the sound of tiny scurrying feet. Mice he guessed, or worse.

There was a glow up ahead. As they walked the air became warmer, less damp. The walls of the tunnel weren't as moist.

They passed the mouth of a cave and Frogboy pointed to it. "Over there's the fire room," he whispered. "Got it's own kind of magic. It can change you every which way. Melt you down, burn you up. Flickering like fire itself. But it's undependable. Go for that kind of magic and you might end up some place you don't want to be."

"Like where?" Sam asked.

"Might get what you want, or, end up toasted like a grilled cheese sandwich," Frogboy replied.

Franklin whispered, "Let's try the magic pool first and if that doesn't—"

"Shhh," Frogboy said, holding his fingers to his lips. "Hear that? Follow me fellas."

Frogboy led them past the opening of the fire room to a side grotto. "In here."

Franklin and Sam crowded in with Frogboy. Frogboy nodded to the narrow, rocky ledges in the cramped cave. Sam saw scores of eyes shining in the low candlelight.

"My cousins," Frogboy whispered. "If I were you guys, I'd do some transforming right now. Take your pick, salamander or frog. I've got an idea how we can get past those birds. That's Rufus and Marly comin' our way if my ears ain't lyin' to me. Gimme your candle, Sam."

Franklin's mouth was tight and serious. He nodded to Sam.

Sam handed his candle to Frogboy and stared at a dark purple salamander with yellow spots down its back. It didn't shrink from his gaze. Sam felt himself contracting. His face stretched, his mouth widened. Then he was on the cool, damp floor of the cave. His chest rose and fell, breathing. But he was breathing with his skin too! Taking in the moist air, refreshed. He looked up at Frogboy, he was huge. Frogboy gave Sam the once over and grinned. Sam glanced at a stocky green frog with great bulging eyes near Frogboy's feet. "What now?" the frog said.

It was Franklin!

Frogboy gently picked the two of them up and put them in his coat pockets. "Shhh...don't make a sound. Let me do the talking."

Frogboy tried to remain calm as he stepped into the main tunnel and headed for the magic pool. His shoulders were wound up tight as a ball of twine.

The two men came up and walked behind him.

Sam was disoriented inside Frogboy's pocket. He couldn't see a thing but he heard footsteps plain as could be.

Frogboy walked faster. Marly slid his walking stick in front of Frogboy and tripped him. Frogboy dropped the candle and went down like a sack of wet laundry. He held out his hands in front of him to cushion the blow so neither Franklin nor Sam were hurt. Unfortunately, Franklin popped out of Frogboy's pocket and landed with a plop on his belly on a cracked railroad tie.

"Well, well, well," Marly said. "If my crow eyes don't deceive me. Looks like our old pal Frogboy, eh Rufus? A street urchin if I ever laid eyes on one."

Rufus peered at the boy on his knees. "I see you haven't made much progress have you, Frogboy? Still the same half-frog, half-boy."

"You should talk," Frogboy said, picking up Franklin with one hand and the candle stump with the other.

Marly tapped his stick on the ground near Frogboy. "Goodness… another child of the streets with no respect for his elders."

"You didn't have to trip me," Frogboy said, as he put the unlit candle in his pants pocket and brushed pebbles off his knees. He was

about to put Franklin back in his coat pocket when Marly stepped
closer, tapped him on the shoulder and said:

"What have we here? A frog with a *pet* frog. Seems a little fishy,
don't it Rufus?"

"Or *froggy*," Rufus replied, laughing low and raspy.

"Who is he?" Marly said, studying Franklin as Rufus held the lantern up over the silent frog. "And what do you have in that other coat
pocket, eh? Thought I saw it move. Looks a little lumpy to me."

"C'mon Frogboy," Rufus said, "out with it. Show us what you got
in your pocket."

Frogboy's forehead was hot as a stove lid. Sweat popped out on his
brow. He felt like any moment it might drip stinging into his eyes and
blind him.

"C'mon," Marly urged.

Frogboy reached in his pocket and pulled Sam out. Sam lay in the
flat of his friend's hand with the light wobbling over him and thought
he might explode from the stress.

"You didn't answer," Rufus said. "Who *are* they?"

"C...cousins," Frogboy stammered. "This one's Jimmy," he nodded to Franklin, "and this one's Joey."

"Cousins eh?" Rufus said. He winked at Marly. "Kissin' cousins?"

"No. On my Ma's side of the family I—"

Marly looked Frogboy in the eye. "I wanta *hold* one of your cousins." His voice was sharp as a blade.

"I don't know, I—"

"I want to hold Jimmy," Marly said, louder this time.

"I...uh...OK," Frogboy replied, trembling. He reluctantly extended his hand with Franklin in it and winced.

Marly leaned his stick against the wall and put Franklin in his
outstretched palm. "That's better. Now you showin' you got good
sense, Frogboy, I—" Marly let out a yelp and dropped Franklin on the
ground. He landed with a thick plop. Marly shook his hand like a dish
rag. "Little bugger peed all over my hand!" He wiped his hand on his

pant leg, grabbed his walking stick and raised it over Franklin. "Why, I oughta—"

"Stop!" Frogboy shouted. He dropped to his knees, scooped Franklin up with his hand and returned him to his pocket. He got back on his feet, stared at Marly with tears in his eyes and slipped Sam in his other pocket. "I never done nothin' to you."

Marly shook his stick in the air and sneered at Frogboy. Frogboy stood still, his feet planted on the ground. His hands were shaking and tears rolled down his cheeks.

Rufus took hold of Marly's stick and pulled it back. "Let him be, Marly. They're his *cousins*. See what you've done? You've upset the boy."

Frogboy stood his ground. His mouth quivered as if he was struggling to speak. Nothing came out.

Marly lowered his stick. "Alright." He raised his hand as if he might say something but stopped in mid-air. "You just tell your cousin he needs to learn some manners, y'hear?"

Frogboy said nothing.

"C'mon man," Rufus said, tapping Marly on the elbow, "we got work to do. Gotta find Sam and that crazy spider friend of his 'fore they high-tail it outta here."

Marly spat on the ground and glared at Frogboy. "Alright," he nodded to Rufus, "let's go."

24

Frogboy watched the backs of the men as they walked away, their shadows wobbled in the low light as if they were drunk. He took the candle from his pants pocket and lit it off one of the lanterns in the wall of the tunnel.

"They gone yet?" Franklin wheezed from Frogboy's pocket. "Lemme out. I can barely breathe in here."

Frogboy lifted Sam and Franklin lightly from his pockets, knelt down and placed them on the cool ground.

Franklin shivered and croaked. "That idiot nearly killed me. Sheesh. Well…if I *was* dead, 'least you wouldn't have to listen to my bellyachin'."

Sam shuddered. "I'd be sad and miss you."

Franklin looked at the boy. "Right—I was kidding. We've gotta outsmart those birds. First thing's first."

Franklin shut his eyes and focused on his breath. Sam could hear nothing in the tunnel but the distant drip of water somewhere.

Franklin stretched and grew, expanding like a thick, sturdy tree until he was back. He stood, blinked, and shook his head in wonder.

Sam took his eyes off Franklin and closed them. He remembered his father, a spatula in his hand with a blueberry pancake on it tossing it in the air like he was a cowboy in the old west. He smiled. "How many of these do you want, Sam?" "Four," Sam replied. "Four it is, for the young cowpuncher," his father said, flipping the cake onto the plate and three more from the cast iron skillet.

Sam breathed in and out and heard a soft whistling sound come from his nostrils. He was throbbing like a great rubber band. His muscles twanging, bones creaking, vertebrae rippling like a garter snake weaving through the grass. His hands filled out and the skin stretched over his flesh like a balloon. He felt the heaviness of bones growing through his arms, down his legs, and out like tree limbs reaching, lengthening and finally stopping.

He was back to Sam.

"Whew!" he said. "Didn't know if we'd make it. Those guys are nuts."

"We'll steer clear of them if we can, deal with them if we must," Franklin said. He put his hand on Frogboy's shoulder. "Thanks...you saved my life. If you hadn't jumped in and helped I'd be a bloody mess by now."

"We've got to stick together," Frogboy replied. "*All* of us."

"That's the spirit, son," Franklin said, letting go of Frogboy's shoulder. "How about you lead us to that beautiful pool? That beautiful *magic* pool."

Sam looked Frogboy in the eye. "They probably would have killed me too...thanks."

Frogboy nodded, paused for a moment in thought and said, "This way men, it's not far."

Frogboy led the way through the dark tunnel. They seemed to be going higher, Sam thought. He watched the railroad ties closely so he wouldn't trip and listened for sounds that might mean trouble.

They passed the openings of several caves on either side of the tunnel.

"What's that one?" Sam asked.

"The Green Room," Frogboy said. "Not bad, but not for everyone. Go in there and you turn green. I always figured I was green enough as it was."

"And that one?" Sam whispered, pointing to another cave.

"Red Room," Frogboy answered. "Enter it and your whole life turns red. Some folks think it's the greatest but I never cared for it."

At last they came to a place where the tunnel turned off. There was a wide-mouthed cave to their right. Frogboy nodded. "This is it."

He led the way. In the darkness up ahead Sam could see a silver, shimmering disk on the ground. Must be the pool, he thought.

They walked to the edge of it and stood, quiet for a moment. Frogboy held the candle over the water. They could see their reflections, three beings peering over the edge. It was clear. There wasn't even a ripple on the surface.

"How deep is it?" Sam asked.

"Put your hand in," Frogboy said.

Sam rolled up his sleeve and stuck his hand in the water. He sank nearly to his shoulder, surprised when he touched the sandy bottom. It was smooth and cool, not cold. "Jeeze, it's not that deep, only a couple feet."

"It's not how deep it is, it's how *deep* it is," Franklin said.

Frogboy nodded.

"I don't get it," Sam said. "My arm feels all tingly though."

"He means, since it's magic, it doesn't matter how deep it is," Frogboy whispered. "It's what's in the water that counts."

"Oh," Sam answered, still confused.

"Shhh," Frogboy said. "I hear something. I don't know if it's those two jackasses, Marly and Rufus. Look!" He pointed past the pool.

"What is it?" Sam asked. Franklin squinted in the darkness.

"Y'see that faint edge over there, a different shade of blue?" Frogboy asked.

"I see something," Sam replied. "Can't tell what it is."

"You're lookin' at sky, Sam. Remember I told you in one of the caves there was a hole in the rock over the river? Listen, we gotta work quickly. I've got a plan. Franklin, you see that great big boulder there?"

Franklin nodded.

"Get behind it. I'm gonna take Sam with me."

"OK," Franklin said quietly, heading for the dark outline of the boulder about ten feet from the pool. He crouched behind it, looked at Frogboy and Sam and smiled. Then his head disappeared behind the craggy black shape.

"Come with me," Frogboy said to Sam, taking his hand, "quick, before they get here."

Sam was nervous but followed Frogboy past the lip of the pool toward the faint sky edge he pointed out. When Sam got closer, he could see the opening was arched, round and rough. The outside night air was cool on his arms. There was a sprinkle of stars in the sky and dark mountain shapes in the distance.

Frogboy stopped with their backs to the cave and let go of Sam's hand. "Look down but don't move."

Sam did. He was standing on a rocky lip. About a hundred feet below was the river. It was ragged-looking and wild. A great black valley spread out before them. He heard the water swirling and crashing over boulders. "Jeeze, Frogboy," he whispered hoarsely, "you don't expect me to jump do you?"

Frogboy smiled. "No, my friend. See that ledge a couple of feet below us?"

"It's narrow," Sam said, looking down over the tops of his shoes.

"That's right, but it will have to do. C'mon Sam, you can do it. We gotta crouch down low and hide on the ledge so those boys don't see us."

He tapped Sam lightly on the elbow, jerked his head and whispered, "They'll be here any minute. We ain't got much time."

Frogboy jumped and Sam held his breath, he couldn't look. When he heard Frogboy's feet land on the ledge below he opened his eyes.

"OK," Frogboy said, "you don't have to jump, just step down."

The ledge was about a foot and a half wide and three feet from the top. Sam was terrified. He took hold of Frogboy's hand, teetered on the edge and stepped into space. His mind was blank as he lowered his foot. He let out a sigh of relief when his sneaker hit the rocky ledge.

"Duck," Frogboy cautioned, tapping Sam on the shoulder. "They're comin'. And, like I said, don't look down."

Sam crouched low with Frogboy and gripped a rock that was sticking out. His heart beat like a hummingbird's wings. He felt like it might burst from his rib cage and zoom to the moon any minute. He listened to the water pound the rocks below and glanced over his shoulder, astonished. Across the dark valley the moon rose up and glowed like the top of a great pail of milk. And the rocks! The rocks below him looked like a miniature mountain range, shadowy and jagged. As if huge boulders had fallen from the sky and landed in a heap on the banks of the river.

He heard footsteps in the room above and froze.

"There's the pool," a voice said, "magic they say."

It was Marly! A chill ran through Sam's body. His tennis shoe tapped out a crazy rhythm on the rocky ledge.

"Looks nice," Rufus answered, "but magic? Who sez? Probably a bunch 'a crazies, that's who."

Sam felt Frogboy move beside him, glanced over and realized to his horror Frogboy was standing up, looking at the two men!

"I'm with you," Marly replied. "I mean, give me a—" he saw Frogboy and yelped, "it's him! That crazy little—"

Sam froze. Frogboy stuffed his thumbs in his ears, fanned his fingers, wiggled them and stuck out his tongue at the men. "Thbbpt," he brazzed.

"Leave that creep to me," Rufus snapped, as he stepped around the pool. He came at Frogboy at a dead run.

Frogboy ducked just as Rufus's feet hit the edge of the cliff. When he realized there was nothing before him but space, he flapped in the air like a large clumsy bird that had been shot. It didn't help, he was going too fast to stop.

"Aiiieeee!" he screamed, plummeting head over heels through the air and landed with a tremendous splash in the churning water below.

Sam glanced down and saw his head bobbing in the water, going downstream.

Then, before he could catch his breath, he caught a yellow glow over his shoulder out the corner of his eye. It was Marly! He knelt, set the lamp down and peered over the ledge at the two boys.

"Heh, heh, heh. Pretty sneaky, Frogboy. And what have we here? Sam too. Thought you could outsmart old Marly, did you? We'll see about that."

He reached down, grabbed Frogboy's arm and pulled, lifting

Frogboy up toward him. "Gotcha," he snarled. "Won't get away from me now you little rat."

Frogboy kicked and screamed as Marly yanked him up. "Do something, Sam. Help me!" he yelled.

Sam was beside himself. He crouched, his mind a jumble of possibilities. What to do? Grab Marly's foot and pull? Get behind him and push? What about Frogboy, then he'd go over the ledge too.

Marly wobbled and nearly slipped. He bent over the lip of the cliff with his hands under Frogboy's arms and struggled to pull him up.

Without thinking, Sam stood up, grabbed hold of one of Marly's arms with both hands and pulled it toward him. Then he bit Marly on the arm as hard as he could and ducked down.

Marly screeched and let go of Frogboy. He teetered and slipped from Marly's hands. Marly stared at his arm in shock. "You bit me, you devil." He shook his arm to get the feeling back, squatted down and reached for Sam.

Sam noticed Franklin creeping up slowly behind Marly. The old man's face was grim and concentrated. He placed his boot on Marly's back, put the weight of his body behind it and shoved with all his might.

Sam saw the terror in Marly's eyes as he flew off the cliff overhead. Marly was a spinning jumble of arms and legs, tumbling, kicking furiously in mid-air.

"Yieeeeeeeeee," he howled, as he shot through the darkness and hit the water below with a cannonball whump.

Sam glanced at Marly as he bobbed in the water. He couldn't see Rufus. The current carried Marly downstream at a brisk clip.

"Where is—" Sam said, looking around, frantic.

"Here—right here!" Frogboy yelped. "Help me, Sam. I'm holding on with all I got. 'Bout to lose it and follow those boys down."

Sam looked down and saw Frogboy's fingers slipping over the wet rock on the ledge.

"I can't—" Frogboy managed, clawing the rough rock.

Sam reached down and grabbed his hand. "You're heavy, Frogboy. I don't know if I can—"

"Grab hold of my hand," Franklin shouted. He knelt on the ledge above the boys. The lantern was at his feet and his face wobbled in the low, yellow light.

Sam glanced at Frogboy. His mouth quivering, scared. Sam kept his grip on Frogboy and brought his other hand up over his head.

Franklin took it with both hands and pulled, sturdy as a post. Frogboy got his feet up on the narrow ledge and Sam tugged with all his might. Then Frogboy was up, standing beside Sam, shaky, hugging him. "You did it, Sam. You *did* it. You saved me!"

Sam held him for a moment and then said, "OK, buddy, it's OK. Let's get to the top before one of us falls off."

Frogboy wiped his eyes with the back of his hand. "Yeah, sure... right." He looked up at Franklin.

The old man was smiling, his brow furrowed and wet with sweat. He shook his head in disbelief. "Jeeze, that was close. You two youngins get on up here. I gotta find my heart. It must be close by. I think it jumped clear outta my chest. Maybe it's behind that rock."

25

Franklin knelt down, lifted the lantern in his hand and peered over the side of the cliff as if the light from it might show him where Marly and Rufus were. "Sheesh, can't see those scoundrels. Don't know if they're alive, or already on the other shore."

Sam climbed up and stood beside Franklin. "Other shore?" he asked, looking over the side.

"Dead," Franklin answered. He stood and brushed the gravel from his knees. "At least they're out of our hair. I doubt they'll come back here and mess with us. If they do…I'll fix 'em for good."

Franklin walked over to the pool and stared at its smooth surface.

Frogboy clambered back up from the ledge, came over to Franklin with a serious look on his face and threw his arms around the man.

"Whoa, what's this?" Franklin said, surprised at the hug.

"You saved my life," Frogboy answered, glancing over his shoulder at Sam, "*both* of you."

Franklin patted Frogboy's head as he let go. "Almost got flattened back there myself."

The three of them stared at the pool for a moment, silent, as if hypnotized by its glassy surface.

Sam looked at Franklin. "Well, what do you think?"

"Think it's time we tried it. See if it's got those magical properties."

"What about me?" Frogboy said, suddenly. His eyes were big and red-rimmed. "I mean, you know, I always wanted to be a boy. A *full* boy, not just a half or a part of one...you know—"

"OK," Franklin said softly. "If there's magic in this pool, there's probably enough to go around."

"How should I do it?" Frogboy asked, looking at Franklin.

"Think about the boy you want to be," Franklin answered. "Think of your face, eyes, hair, nose, mouth. Don't think of any boy you've ever seen. That's not you. Don't think of me or Sam—*you*. Your eyes, your hair, your ears."

"OK," Frogboy said.

"Wade in and lie face down," Franklin said. "Don't know if this will work or not, but we might as well try."

"But what if I—" Frogboy protested.

"You don't know," Franklin answered firmly. "Maybe nothing will happen. The only way you'll find out is, *go*...go *in*...immerse. Do it with all your heart, body and mind. No more of this half and half stuff. Remember, you want to be a wholehearted boy, don't you?"

Frogboy nodded. He stared at the pool for a moment. Sam noticed his hands were shaking, knees too. "OK, fellas," Frogboy said at last. He gripped Sam's hand tight and shook it. Then he turned to Franklin and did the same.

"Try," Franklin said, quietly, when Frogboy let his hand go.

Frogboy stood at the edge of the pool and closed his eyes for a moment. Sam saw his lips move but couldn't hear any words. Then, Frogboy opened his eyes and walked slowly in. When he was halfway across, he dropped to his knees, took a deep breath and lowered the rest of his body until he was floating face down.

He stayed like that for a while, not moving. Sam's palms were moist and his heart thumped wildly in his chest. He looked across the pool at Franklin. "D'you think?"

Franklin shook his head.

There was the sound of bubbles popping up from both sides of Frogboy's head. A few at first, followed by a great foaming mass. Then they stopped.

Franklin stepped into the pool, lifted Frogboy out of the water and set him down on the side, soaking wet.

Sam stared in disbelief. He no longer had the face of a frog. On top of his head was a mass of soggy dark blonde hair. Water ran down his face. His eyes were shut. Sam couldn't tell if he was alive.

Franklin gently shook Frogboy and slapped his cheeks lightly with the flat of his hand. "Frogboy—wake up, it's us. Franklin and Sam."

Sam rushed over and knelt by his side. "Say something, Frogboy!" he yelled.

Frogboy blinked and opened his eyes. "Something. Something loud in my ear."

"You did it, Frogboy, you did it!" Sam shook his head in amazement. He jumped up and danced a jig, flapping his arms like the wings of a crazy chicken. He smacked his knee with the flat of his hand and laughed, a raw, joyous laugh. "I can't believe you did it. You're a boy!"

Frogboy was stunned. He stared at Sam like he'd just dropped from the sky. He blinked again and felt his nose with his fingertips. Then ran them over his eyes. "I've got eyebrows," he said, astonished, "and a nose—a real nose!"

"Look," Franklin said, nodding to the pool.

Frogboy scrambled to the edge and peered over. Franklin and Sam knelt beside him until there were three faces hovering over the smooth surface. Frogboy put his hands to his cheeks and shook his head gently. "Wow. All I can say is—wow."

Franklin clapped him on the shoulder. "Glad you made it back. Thought you might be gone for good. Maybe you went all the way back and became a frog. All those bubbles around your head."

"I was gone," Frogboy said. "I don't know if I could describe it, but...some part of me was going away...leaving...*dying*."

"And some part of you came back," Sam said, punching Frogboy lightly on the shoulder.

"There's one other thing we need to do for you Frogboy," Franklin said. "'Course you don't *have* to do it, but...I'd recommend it."

"What's that?" Frogboy asked.

"Your name," Franklin said. "I think you should have a new one."

"Oh yeah," Frogboy said, looking thoughtful. "Well, I…don't have any ideas in my brand new head. I've been Frogboy for so long, I don't know…."

Sam stared at the pool as if a name might rise up out of the water and strike him in the forehead.

"Where are you?" Franklin said to Sam. "Looks like you're a million miles away."

Sam shook his head and glanced at Franklin's craggy face in the low light. "I was thinking of my Dad. I remember him telling me after we read bedtime stories one night he wished he had another."

"Another what?" Frogboy said.

"Another boy or girl," Sam said. "So he could have a spare."

"Whoa," Frogboy said.

"He said it as a joke I think," Sam continued, "but they seriously wished they had another. Had a name picked out for a boy and a girl. My mom and he were thinking of having another kid, but of course they didn't. They broke up." Sam stared at the sandy bottom of the water. "Dad said he was glad they got one out of the deal."

"What was the name?" Franklin asked.

"If I had a sister, her name would've been Isobel," Sam said, still looking at the water, "and a brother?" He stopped for a moment to bring the memory up like a minnow from the bottom. "If I had a brother they were going to call him…Henry."

Franklin looked at Frogboy. He gazed in the pool too, eyes half-closed, listening to Sam. "Look here," Franklin said, tapping Frogboy on the shoulder. "Unless these old eyes and ears deceive me, I believe you just got a name, courtesy your friend and mine, Sam."

"What?" Frogboy said, a dazed look in his eyes.

"Why, Henry," Franklin said, smacking Frogboy on the back. "It's a good strong name, regal even, and, as a bonus, if it's a little too long you can call yourself Hank."

"Wow," Frogboy exclaimed, "it's like having two names."

"Yeah, pretty cool," Sam said, smiling.

Franklin turned solemn and knelt before Frogboy. "On your knees, my boy, and I do mean boy, and face me."

Frogboy did as Franklin asked.

Franklin held up his right hand and said, "With all the powers vested in me as a wholehearted creature walking the face of this great earth, I now pronounce you Henry...Hank for short." Then he placed his palm lightly on Frogboy's head and let it go.

He stared at Franklin for a moment and then said his name softly. "Henry."

"Atta boy," Franklin said, "you're getting the hang of it."

Sam cleared his throat. Henry and Franklin looked at him. "Ahem. I...I...don't want to interrupt this happy celebration, but I want to go back home. I don't know if this magic will work for me, but I'm ready to try." He looked at Franklin. "Can I?"

Franklin nodded, slapped his leg with his hand and stood up. "My apologies, Sam. You've been patient—*more* than patient."

Sam turned to Franklin. "How should I *do* this?"

"Stand here by me," Franklin said, motioning to Sam. Sam got up and stood by him. "I want you to think about your mother and father, your life with them. Then close your eyes and *dive* into the pool."

Sam blinked and stared at Franklin in disbelief. "It's...it's only a few feet deep. What if I—"

"I know," Franklin said, his face serious. "You'll be taking a leap. A leap like the one that brought you into this world. The difference is, this one's on purpose. You're taking a leap of faith."

Sam took a deep breath and walked to the edge of the pool. Henry stood up and gave him room.

Sam took a step forward.

"Wait!" Franklin said. "I want to sing something to send you on your way."

Sam turned and looked at him, not sure what he meant.

Without waiting, Franklin took a step forward, closed his eyes and began to sing:

Our fathers crossed over the river
They're now in the kingdom, it's true
They're now in the kingdom where all of us dwell
Go wash in that beautiful pool

Our mothers crossed over the river
They're now in the kingdom, it's true
They're now in the kingdom where all of us dwell
Go wash in that beautiful pool

Go wash in that beautiful pool
Go wash in that beautiful pool
The river is wide and flowing through you
Go wash in that beautiful pool

When he was finished, Franklin blinked and nodded to Sam.

Sam felt something rushing up in him that had no name. It was like gratitude but somehow bigger. It came from a place of no words. An enormous space that didn't seem to have a beginning or end and no edges anywhere.

Sam turned to Henry and shook his hand. "Goodbye, Fr—I mean Henry. It's great to be a boy. You'll have more adventures than you could ever imagine. But sometimes...you might wish you were a frog again."

Henry shook his head, puzzled.

"It's probably less complicated than this," Sam said, hooking his thumb to his chest.

Franklin came up and gave Sam a hug. He was sturdy as an oak, with his limbs wrapped around the boy. Feeling flew up in Sam's heart like a flock of birds, a confusion of wings, his heart beating in mid-air to stay aloft.

Franklin released him.

Sam looked at the old man. "It's hard to—"

Franklin touched him lightly on the shoulder. "Go."

Sam glanced at his friends one more time, stood up straight and faced the pool. He closed his eyes, pressed his hands together before his chest and dove.

He expected to hit the sandy bottom and have to try again, perhaps a few times to get it right. Maybe Franklin was wrong, maybe he needed to perfect his technique. But he felt nothing but water; smooth, strong, carrying him deeper, lower. It's as if he didn't have clothes on, or skin, or bones. He was water sinking into water, melting effortlessly. He was dark and blue and quiet.

Then he felt a tap on his forehead, a little sandy.

Must be the bottom he thought.

26

S am blinked.

There was his father's face, hovering over him. His eyes big, brown and worried. And the room—white this and white that. Clean as could be. Even white light blasting in the windows.

He blinked again.

His father's face rippled for a moment above him as if he was coming up from the bottom of a stream. His mouth quivered between sadness, uncertainty and joy, and then collapsed into something that looked like relief.

"Dad!" Sam shouted. He lunged for his father, arms outstretched.

His father put his hands on Sam's shoulders and held him back. Then he bent over, wrapped his arms around the boy and crushed him in a hug.

"You're back, Sam…back," his father said, his chest heaving. "I thought I'd lost you, son. Let me look at you." His father pulled away and couldn't speak for a moment. Then wrapped his arms around Sam and hugged him again, this time more gently.

When they separated Sam said, "Where am I?"

"The hospital." His father nodded to the tube in Sam's arm. "That's why I couldn't let you get up, just now. Doc says you're dehydrated."

"I'm what?"

His father laughed and patted Sam's knee. "You need fluids."

"How did I get here?"

"I…we, found you. Late last night in that cellar. Actually, it was that bloodhound Buster that did it. I thought that dog was a washed-up bag of bones when the policeman brought him to the cabin. He wheezed like an old man, snuffling on the floor with his big wet nose. But he did it, he really did. That old hound *found* you."

"Am I in trouble?"

His father shook his head. "No, no, no. You might get a lecture from the policeman, but that's the least of your worries. He's kind of an odd duck really, short, sturdy and thick as a stump. Name's Frank. But, I gotta say, he and that dog, what a team. I gave Buster one of your old T-shirts and he shook it like a rag doll and kept it in his mouth the whole time he was tracking you. Found that field you went through and the old farmhouse too. It was dark, we could barely see. Buster went up and down the stairs in the house when we got there. Then he found the cellar door. Took three steps and paused. Frank and I were impatient, like, 'c'mon pooch, let's go.' Buster knew what he was doing. Frank shined a light down the stairs and there you were."

Sam's father paused, stared out the window for a moment and then continued softly, "I didn't know…wasn't sure…hoped you were still…."

Sam's eyes widened. "I met someone named Franklin. He was kinda short and sturdy. Helped me out, Frogboy too. Taught me things, how to change into things and change back, that's what he said. He said, 'Sam, you can become anything you want, but you've got to come back.' I turned into a bird and there were these two men, not men really, but they had the heads of crows and bodies of men.

Named Marly and Rufus. They captured me, put me in a cage, Dad, and Franklin *helped* me. Turned into a spider and picked the lock. I saw him at the circus with the Lioness Von Baroness of Pyromania."

His father squeezed Sam's hand and nodded. "That was some fall. You've got quite a goose egg on your forehead." He touched Sam's forehead lightly with his fingertips. "How does it feel?"

"Ouch." Sam ran his fingers over the lump. It was a rough, sandy scab, still tender. "Hurts some." He stopped touching his head and looked at his dad. "You don't believe me, do you?"

"No Sam, I never said I—"

"You *gotta* believe me, Dad." Sam's voice rose up like a bird. "There was a tree that could talk. A ballerina dancing on the hand of a buffalo man. I met this…this…nutty talking squirrel named Chester. He was looking for his dad, named Emmett—can you believe it? And Rubberface, what a scary guy he was. Tried to chop down a tree with Chester and Florence in it and…and…I *saved* 'em. Turned into a hawk and put them on my back and flew down to safety and the tree…the tree fell on Rubberface."

His father took Sam's hand and brought it to his cheek. Sam thought his father might cry right then. "You did a good thing, son, to save those squirrels. That was a wonderful thing. I hope they thanked you."

There was a sharp sound like someone hitting a ring on the door. Sam and his father turned. A man stood in the doorway in a white coat and pale blue hospital pants. He held a clipboard in his hand and tapped the door again with the flat of his hand even though he had their attention. He smiled broadly, a mouthful of white teeth. "Well, look who's up."

He strode across the room and stood beside Sam's father who was still sitting on the bed. Sam's father looked dazed for a moment and then said, "Sorry…this is Doctor Roswell. He's been a tremendous help when we found—"

"I'm so glad you're back with us, Sam," the doctor interrupted. He reached out, picked up Sam's hand and shook it firmly. His eyes were blue as his pants. He stared intently into Sam's eyes as if he was looking for something and then dropped the boy's hand. "My name is Dr. Roswell, but you can call me Henry if you like."

"Uh…OK." Sam almost said something else but stopped himself.

The doctor, his smile gone, turned to Sam's father. "Can I please have a word with you, Mr. Bixby?" He nodded to the hallway.

"I hate to leave him for a moment after what he's been through."

"We'll leave the door open so you can keep an eye on him," the doctor said. "I need to discuss, *you* know…" He cocked his head to the door.

"Alright," Sam's father said, letting the air out of his lungs in a sigh, "but only for a moment." He got up and clutched Sam's hand, as the doctor left the room. "I'll be right back. Don't go anywhere. I'm kidding, but I'm *not* kidding. I mean, don't go scampering off to any abandoned farmhouses."

"I won't." He let go of his father's hand and watched the back of his head as he disappeared through the doorway.

When they were out in the hallway the doctor turned to Sam's father. "I need to ask your son some questions."

"Questions?"

"To determine if there's been a concussion or not. And, if there is…if he's in any danger."

Sam's father looked as if someone punched him in the stomach. His mouth was a tight line. Finally, he said, "OK, if you have to."

"I have to. He looks fine, but these things aren't always as simple as they seem. Sometimes patients look like they're out of the woods and…they're *not*, if you follow me."

"I follow you." Sam's father stared at the door of Sam's room. "He's been telling me these…these…wild tales. Stuff about guys named Franklin, Rubberface, Chester. Talking squirrels, people turning into spiders. Yeesh…I hope he's OK and can get back to some kind of normal soon."

The doctor held up the clipboard and tapped it with a pencil he pulled from the clip. "Normal. Well…I guess everyone has a different idea of what *that* is." With the pencil's eraser, he pointed to a piece of lined note paper with messy handwriting on it.

"What's that?"

"The contents of Sam's stomach," the doctor said. "You know we had to pump it to find out if there was some poison or something. I don't know what stories he's been telling you, but there are some things here I've never seen in a boy's stomach."

"Like what?"

"Well, some of these are perfectly normal: blackberry pie, milk, some kind of bread, cherries."

"I didn't give him those," Sam's father said, a puzzled expression on his face.

"Wait, there's more. We're still doing tests on this stuff. Let's see, some kind of pig I guess, and here's the kicker; we found six tadpoles, a waterborne insect, and a few other things we're having the lab look at."

"Good heavens. Do you think that these things caused his…his wild flights of fancy? Maybe he's still a little light in the head from the fall."

The doctor shook his head. "I know you want something definite, Mr. Bixby but we just don't have that yet. Like I said, we've got to do some more tests, and—"

"DAAAD!"

His father jerked as if someone shot a dart into him. He rushed into the room, sat down on the bed and took Sam's hand in his. He looked in Sam's eyes. The boy was spooked. "For heaven's sake honey, what's wrong? Did something scare you?"

Sam stared at the clear plastic tube leading from his arm to the hanging drip on the metal pole as if he'd noticed it for the first time and then looked back at his dad. "Nectar," he said. "Just like a honey-bee." A smile crept across his face.

Sam put his arms around his father. "I didn't know where you were. Now that I'm back I want you here, close by, so I can *see* you. Keep an eye on you, like you say. You know?"

His father wrapped Sam in a bear hug. A wave of relief rolled over him. His shoulders shook. They had been tight ever since Sam disappeared. Then his father let go, a long breath, a great sigh that whistled softly in Sam's ear.

"I know, son…I know."

ABOUT THE AUTHOR

Brett Gadbois was born in Kankakee, Illinois and grew up near Minneapolis, Minnesota. His short stories have appeared in various literary journals. His story *Perfect* was nominated for the Pushcart Prize.

He lives with his son on Bainbridge Island, Washington.

⌒

ABOUT THE ILLUSTRATOR

Nicolas Gadbois was born in Iowa City, Iowa and grew up near Minneapolis, Minnesota. He is a fine artist working in paint and concrete. He has illustrated a number of children's books.

He lives near Santa Fe, New Mexico.

⌒

QUICK ORDER FORM

Email orders: bgadbois@sounddsl.com

Postal Orders: Belltown Press, Brett Gadbois, 11190 Forest Lane NE, 98110. Bainbridge Island, WA

Please send the following book.

_____

Your information here:

Name: _____

Address: _____

City: _____ State: _____ Zip: _____

Telephone: _____

Email address: _____

Sales tax: Please add 8.6% for products shipped to Washington state addresses.

Shipping by air

U.S: $4.00 for first book and $2.00 for each additional book.

International: $9.00 for each book and $5.00 for each additional book.

BELLTOWN
PRESS